I0738479

WHISKEY FLIGHT

CEDAR CREEK SUSPENSE, VOLUME 1

VIOLET HOWE

This is a work of fiction. The characters, incidents, events, and dialogues in this book are of the author's imagination and are not to be construed as real. Any resemblance to actual events or persons, living or dead, is completely coincidental.

No part of this book may be reproduced or transmitted in any form or by any means, electronic or mechanical, including photocopying, recording, or by any information storage and retrieval system, without permission in writing from the author.

www.violethowe.com

Cover Design: Elizabeth Mackey
www.elizabethmackeygraphics.com

Published by Charbar Productions, LLC
(p-v1)
Copyright © 2020 Violet Howe/LM Howe/Charbar Productions, LLC
All rights reserved.
Print ISBN: 978-1-7327269-1-8

For the Ultra Violets
*Thank you for living in Cedar Creek with me and loving these
characters as much as I do.*

BOOKS BY VIOLET HOWE

<u>**Tales Behind the Veils**</u>

Diary of a Single Wedding Planner

Diary of a Wedding Planner in Love

Diary of an Engaged Wedding Planner

Maggie

<u>**The Cedar Creek Collection**</u>

Cedar Creek Mysteries:

The Ghost in the Curve

The Glow in the Woods

The Phantom in the Footlights

Cedar Creek Families:

Building Fences

Crossing Paths

Cedar Creek Suspense:

Whiskey Flight

<u>**Soul Sisters at Cedar Mountain Lodge**</u>

Christmas Sisters

Christmas Hope

Visit www.violethowe.com to subscribe to Violet's monthly newsletter for news on upcoming releases, events, sales, and other tidbits.

ONE

H it men don't wear name badges, so I didn't know for sure if the stranger in the corner booth had been sent to kill me or if he was just a lonely out-of-towner who'd happened to pick my local bar.

He sat alone, his beer untouched and his attention focused on his phone. His ankle-length chinos stood out in the sea of denim and khakis, and the loafers he wore without socks were a stark contrast to the cowboy boots, work boots, and sneakers on everyone else.

"Hey, Shannon," I said to the bartender as she poured a beer from the tap in front of me. "That guy over there, the one in the corner? Have you ever seen him in here before?"

She glanced up at him and then shook her head.

"Nah. Trust me, I would have remembered him," she said with a grin and a wink. "Definitely not from around here. A city guy, I bet. Probably looking for real estate to scoop up."

I sneaked another peek at him as she walked away to deliver the beer to the other end of the bar.

He looked harmless enough, but I had learned the hard way that I was a bad judge of character.

I didn't even realize my own husband was a hitman with the mob until he'd been arrested.

Even then, I hadn't wanted to believe it was true.

How could the intelligent, sensitive, romantic, and passionate man I'd fallen head over heels in love with be a cold-blooded murderer?

This was a man who would discuss Shakespeare with me until the wee hours of the morning, and then get up early to plant Gerbera daisies in our back garden so my life would have more color. The man who would have a hot bath waiting for me after a long night at the news station where I worked, and who would sit cross-legged on the floor with his niece and her stuffed animals when she invited him to a tea party.

Granted, I'd rushed in. It was the first time in my life I'd ever been swept off my feet, and two weeks to the day after our first date, we got married in a courthouse ceremony and celebrated by dancing barefoot on the candlelit back deck of my house. Two months later, he was behind bars, and I was left alone, numb with shock, grief, and regret.

I rattled the ice cubes in my whiskey and took another sip, allowing the layered flavors of the fiery liquid to open on my tongue.

It had been two years since Victor's arrest, and in many ways, I was still numb. And damned near destitute.

Between my legal fees and the government freezing my assets, I'd almost been bankrupted. My career had abruptly ended, and my sense of identity had been shattered along with my heart. I'd moved back home to Cedar Creek with my tail between my legs, hoping my small, rural hometown where everyone knew everyone would be a safe place to hide and heal.

No place was safe, though. Not even Cedar Creek. The detective who questioned me after Victor's arrest had warned me that I'd likely be under two microscopes—the Mafia's and the government's. Either might have me followed, but only one would put a hit out on me.

Was that why the stranger was in town?

I'd first noticed him about a week earlier in the grocery store. I'd been smelling strawberries, looking for a pint a tad overripe, when he caught my eye.

He'd worn ankle-length chinos that day as well, gray instead of black. He'd paired them with a white button-down shirt cut so narrow that it hugged his ribs and threatened to burst at the seams across his pronounced biceps.

As if his metropolitan fashion choices weren't enough to make him stand out in the rural setting, he stood staring at the cilantro and parsley with empty hands, no shopping cart or basket in sight.

When I'd first moved back to Cedar Creek, I'd been jumpy and easily startled, suspicious of everyone and wary of what danger might have followed me home from Chicago.

But after a couple of months with no incidents, I began to relax a little. I convinced myself the Mafia had no need to come after me. I'd proven I didn't know anything, that I wasn't any kind of threat. I told myself that they had no reason to kill me.

The stranger brought my paranoia back though, and my instinct that first day I saw him had been to put distance between us.

I left the strawberries behind and moved to a different aisle, glancing over my shoulder every couple of seconds to see if he was behind me. I considered abandoning my cart and heading outside, but I worried he might follow me to my car, and I felt safer indoors in the company of other people.

Twice more I spotted him as I hastened to grab the few items I needed. He didn't seem to notice me. He never made eye contact or came closer to me, but I couldn't shake the feeling that his presence was connected to me.

Though I was hesitant to leave the relative safety of the store, I had no proof that he meant me harm, so eventually, I made my way to my car. I sat and waited, and sure enough, within a couple of minutes of my exit, he walked out into the sunlight, adjusting his shades down over his eyes from their perch on the top of his head.

Who walks through an entire grocery store, aisle by aisle, and leaves with nothing? Not even a candy bar?

I'd kept an eye out for him in the days that followed, but I hadn't seen him again until tonight in the bar.

Lost in my thoughts, I hadn't noticed he had looked up and caught me staring. A grin played at the corner of his mouth as I looked away, my face hot with embarrassment.

I preoccupied myself with the peanuts in the bowl in front of me, cracking open a couple of shells to pop the stale, salty nuts into my mouth. I chased them down with a swig of whiskey and then motioned to Shannon that I'd have another glass.

She raised an eyebrow, and I ignored her. It wasn't every day that a woman got a call to let her know her ex-husband was being transferred to a federal prison. Who could fault me for wanting to be a little more numb than usual? I'd walked the three blocks to the bar with the full intention of being unable to drive home. I could stumble that far back if needed.

I tossed a peanut into the air and opened my mouth to catch it, but I missed, and it fell inside my shirt. As I reached to fish it from my cleavage, my elbow made contact with the person about to take the barstool next to me.

"Oh, sorry."

"That's all right," he said. "It was just my arm. I'm sure if you had seen it was me, I'd have a black eye."

Seth Donovan. Quite possibly the last person on earth I wanted to see at that moment. Well, all right, Victor Gallo was the *last* person I wanted to see, but since my ex-husband was in prison, my childhood sweetheart had moved from second place on the list to first.

"Is that whiskey you're drinking?" Seth asked as Shannon placed a full glass in front of me and took away the empty one. "I've never known you to be a hard liquor girl. What are we celebrating?"

"*We* aren't celebrating anything," I said, shifting my weight on the stool to turn away from him. "I'd prefer to drink alone."

"Ouch," he said. "You know, I thought at some point we'd at

least be able to be cordial now that you're back in town. I guess not, and I guess that's my cue to find another seat. Shannon, nice to see you."

He walked away, and Shannon stared at me with a stunned expression.

"What?" I growled.

She held up both hands and shook her head.

"I didn't say a word. My lips are sealed." With a zipping motion across her mouth, she turned away.

I frowned, embarrassed at my own rudeness. Seth had been nothing but polite each of the three times I'd seen him since moving back to town, and I'd gotten nastier every time.

It wasn't like he'd done anything to deserve it. I was the one who broke things off all those years ago. It was me who'd ended all contact and stopped taking his calls.

At the time, I'd felt betrayed by him. He'd backed out on our plans. He'd refused to run away with me and escape the confines of Cedar Creek.

Now that I'd tasted real betrayal—betrayal so deep and so insidious that it left a black, rotted spot inside my heart—I knew that what Seth had done didn't measure up to that in any way.

The problem was, I'd been angry with Seth for so long that I didn't know how not to be. It kind of blurred into my anger with Victor like a general rage against love and vulnerability. Since Victor wasn't around to catch the brunt of it, Seth made an excellent stand-in target.

"I take it you and the deputy have a history?" Shannon said as she returned to wipe the bar in front of me.

Hmmph. That was an understatement. Seth had been my first crush in kindergarten, my glued-to-the-hip companion throughout elementary, my first kiss in junior high, and a key player in every single memory I had of high school and college. Hell, he was the only serious boyfriend I'd ever had. Not counting Victor, of course, but Victor had gone straight from stranger to spouse so quickly I didn't count him as a boyfriend, and two months of living a lie couldn't be taken seriously.

"A history? Yeah. You could say that," I finally responded over the rim of my glass. "We knew each other when I lived here before. Thirteen years ago."

"Dang. If you're still that mad after thirteen years, he must have really screwed you over. Sucks to hear that. I've always thought Seth was one of the nice guys. I don't know him that well, though. He doesn't come in too often. Just the weekends he's not on duty. All I know is he's not one of those who hits on every girl who walks through the door, and he never gets wasted and acts an ass. Always tips well, too. Calls me by my name. Real respectful."

I swallowed my whiskey and winced at the burn.

"Don't let me change your opinion. Seth *is* a nice guy," I said, coming to his defense in my guilt for somehow casting him in a nega-tive light. "At least, he was when I knew him."

Shannon sighed. "In my experience, men are either good guys at their core, or they're not. They don't tend to change much. I'm sure if you sat down and had a drink with Seth, you'd find he was pretty much the same person you knew him to be. But what do I know?"

A customer beckoned her from farther down the bar, and she smiled with a shrug as she walked away.

I glanced over my shoulder to see if Metro Man was still there, looking away quickly when I saw he was staring at me. I waited a couple of minutes, what seemed like an eternity, and then I turned on the barstool and did a quick scan of the bar, careful to start on the opposite end of where he sat.

The booths along the back wall were all filled with people laugh-ing, talking, drinking, and eating. A typical Friday night out for friends.

A trio of ladies stood near the billiards table watching one man line up his cue stick and take his shot, and his opponent roared with laughter when he missed.

Three dartboards hung on the adjacent wall, and Seth had joined one of the groups tossing darts.

He was more buff now than when I'd known him. Years spent in law enforcement had bulked up his body, making him much more muscular than the scrawny teen of my memories.

Gone were the lustrous locks of his youth. He wore his dark brown hair cut too close to his head to form the wavy curls that I'd loved to twist around my fingers.

His jawline was more chiseled, the angles of his face sharpened by age, but his eyes were still the same soft chocolate brown they'd always been.

Tearing my gaze away from Seth to let it roam over the tables in the center of the room, I finally dared to look toward the stranger.

He was ready this time, waiting for the eye contact, and he lifted his beer in a toast as he grinned and gave me a nod.

I spun away so quickly that I damned near fell off the barstool, and then I propped my elbow on the bar and let my dark hair fall forward to shield my face from his view.

Was he taunting me? Was he letting me know he was aware I knew his purpose?

Or was I overreacting?

There'd been nothing sinister in his glance. It could have been flirtation. What if he wasn't a hitman at all? What if he was simply a guy in a bar hoping to score on a Friday night?

Maybe I should have let Seth sit next to me. That would have at least discouraged any unwanted advances from Metro Man. On the other hand, if my initial instincts about the stranger were correct, associating with me might put Seth in danger, and that was the last thing I wanted to do.

I pulled out my phone to check my emails for a distraction, and as I scrolled through my inbox, Shannon set another whiskey on the bar and smiled.

"Compliments of the snazzy dresser in the corner."

So, it *had* been a come-on. Surely, a hitman wouldn't be so blatantly obvious as to send me a drink and call attention to himself.

Relief flooded through me, followed by the need to squelch any further attention from my new admirer.

"Oh, tell him I'm not interested, please."

"He already paid for it," Shannon said. "You might as well drink it."

She turned her attention to another customer, and I shook my head in frustration.

As happy as I was to discover he wasn't out to kill me, I had no desire to strike up a conversation with him either.

Figuring that a gentle but firm rebuff right off the bat would be the best way to handle the situation, I turned to face his direction, prepared to communicate my disinterest with my eyes and a shake of my head. To my surprise, his booth was empty. A wad of cash lay on the table next to his beer, which still appeared full.

Why would he buy me a drink and then leave? It didn't make sense in either theory of who or what he was.

I hastily scanned the crowd again, unconvinced that he had gone.

"Hey, Shannon? Did that guy say anything when he bought my drink?"

"Nah, not really. Just that he wanted to buy another round for the lady in the red shirt." She looked over toward his booth and frowned. "Where'd he go?"

"Beats me," I said with a shrug. "You're sure you've never seen him in here before?"

"Positive. Like I said, I'd remember him. You know how this place is. We're the local hangout. We get the same people in and out, hardly ever any out-of-towners. Maybe he went to the bathroom. Or maybe he had to take a call and stepped outside. If I see him come back in, I'll give you a heads-up."

"All right. Thanks."

I turned to place my back against the bar so I could watch the bathroom door and the entry door. I didn't want any surprises.

A loud burst of laughter erupted from one of the dart groups, and my eyes were drawn to Seth again. He was laughing with them, his perfect white teeth exposed as he tilted his head to one side to listen to what the guy next to him was saying.

A pang of longing and remembrance hit me, and I tossed back my glass and drained it, trying to find a buffer against the pain.

This would have been my life. This would have been my Friday night. If I had stayed in Cedar Creek and married Seth, I'd be a part of that laughing group. We'd be sharing inside jokes with our friends. He'd have his arm around me, and it would be my voice he'd tilted his head to hear.

Instead, I'd run off to the city in pursuit of excitement and a bigger life than Cedar Creek could offer.

I'd gotten the bigger life, and I'd had my share of excitement since I'd left, but things hadn't turned out exactly the way I'd planned.

Now, here I was, back in my hometown, drinking alone at the bar.

My fast-paced, high-paying career in television news production was over. Instead, I'd thrown myself into opening a community theater to bring the arts to Cedar Creek, but I couldn't even accomplish that. My endeavor had been beset with more roadblocks and obstacles than I ever could have imagined, and I wasn't certain I'd be able to get the theater going at all.

Instead of my posh, renovated house in a trendy Chicago neighborhood with an upscale restaurant or hot-spot bar on every corner, I was living in my late grandmother's two-bedroom clapboard house and walking three blocks to reach a bar that didn't even have a sign out front and only served wings, burgers, fries, and free stale peanuts.

As Seth laughed and celebrated the start of the weekend with his friends, I sat alone—paranoid, fearful, and filled with regrets.

This was not how I had envisioned my life.

Suddenly, I was no longer content to sit on that bar stool and mourn the loss of my dreams, my aspirations, and my ill-fated marriage. I wanted to laugh, too. I wanted to feel good. I wanted life to be normal in some sense, even if just for one night, and even if it was exactly the normal I'd tried to escape.

TWO

"Hey, Shannon? Do you happen to know what Seth's drinking? Can I get one?"

She chuckled with a knowing smile, and I chose to ignore it as I paid her for Seth's beer and gathered up my whiskey, along with my courage, to walk across the bar to his group.

He looked up and made eye contact with me as I approached, and I couldn't tell if the shift in his expression was surprise or trepidation.

"I come in peace," I said, in case it was the latter. "In fact, I bring a peace offering."

I handed him the beer, and he took it with a hesitant grin.

"Is it poisoned?"

"No," I said, pulling the cocktail napkin from beneath the glass in my hand to wave it in front of him. "See? White flag. Truce! Can we talk?"

His eyes narrowed, and I hated that he didn't trust such a simple request from me. I couldn't blame him, though. I'd done that. I'd destroyed a lifetime of friendship. And love.

"Um, sure," he said as he looked around the room. "You wanna get a table?"

"Yeah. I mean, if that's okay. I don't want to take you away from your friends."

"It's fine. Mike and I were losing anyway." He turned to the group and called to one of the guys. "Hey, Kyle, fill in for me for a minute, would ya?"

"No problem," Kyle said, taking Seth's darts.

We walked toward the empty booth that Metro Man had occupied, and as we navigated the tight space of tables and people, Seth's hand brushed against the small of my back ever so briefly to guide me.

It was nothing—a casual touch in no way intimate—but I'd been starved of a man's touch since Victor's arrest a little over two years ago, and this wasn't just any man.

My heart quickened, and memories of Seth filled my head. Our first kiss. Our first touch. Our first time.

His face flushed red as we sat across from each other, and he averted his eyes.

Was he having the same flashbacks? Did they affect him the same way they did me?

"So, what's up?" he asked. "What did you want to talk about?"

I swallowed hard, uncertain of my decision now that it was time to say the words. "I wanted to apologize."

He arched an eyebrow and tilted his head to the left. "Oh? What for?"

"I haven't been the nicest person to you since I got back."

"Really? I hadn't noticed." His sarcasm was heavy and familiar, but his grin gave me hope that it wasn't fueled by anger.

"I've just been going through a lot. It seems like every time I've run into you since I came home, it's been a bad time. A bad time for me, I mean. My life. My circumstances. Not that it was bad to see you."

He stared back at me, silent, like he could see right through me, just as he always had. I crossed my arms over my chest and caved my shoulders a bit, folding in on myself to hide, to keep him from seeing those rotted spots inside me from the horrible mistakes I'd made.

At one time, he'd known me better than anyone, even my own family. He could read me like a book back then, and we had no secrets between us. Nothing hidden.

It struck me how different that was from my whirlwind romance with Victor, which had been all deception, all lies.

Seth grinned again, but his gaze still held mine unchanging. The grin was for appearances. He was trying to keep things lighthearted, but the pain was there in his eyes. Even after thirteen years, I still knew him well enough to know that.

"And here I thought you were going to apologize for disappearing on me," he said. "I've been waiting for that one a while."

Ah, a dagger thrown. A door opened that had long ago been shut. Were we really going to go there? Was it even necessary after all this time? What did it matter anymore?

His attempt at a grin faded with my silence, and he shook his head and looked away.

Evidently, it still mattered to him.

"I'm sorry, Seth."

He took a swig of his beer and stared at the amber liquid once he'd set the glass back down.

"Somehow, I thought hearing that would be a lot more satisfying," he said, his voice quiet. He took a deep breath and then another drink from his glass before he looked at me and grinned again. "So, you're gonna be an aunt, huh? I saw Amy at the store the other day. She seems over the moon."

Grateful for the subject change, I smiled broadly and uncrossed my arms, willing to be open if it meant discussing my sister instead of me.

"Yes. She and Leo are both thrilled, and I'm so happy for them. We're almost done with her nursery, and they've been going to pregnancy classes at Jensen Memorial. I swear, you'd think she's the only woman who's ever been pregnant. Every little thing that happens is monumental."

Seth laughed. "Amy's always been a bit on the dramatic side."

"A bit? That's the understatement of the year. My baby sister came into the world blue, and she's thrived on the drama surrounding her ever since. She's the only person I know who can stub her toe and turn it into a story that has people hanging on the edge of their seat."

"She's hilarious, though. I'd listen to her tell a story about stubbing her toe, and I bet it'd be entertaining as hell. You gotta love her."

"Oh, I do. I adore her to pieces. She's my favorite person on the planet, no doubt."

"Do you remember that time—" He leaned across the table on his elbow, propping his head in his hand as he chuckled. "—you were doing something to her hair, something that was supposed to make it curly?"

"Oh, my God! The home perm from hell!"

We both burst out laughing at the memory of the disaster.

"She looked like a French poodle." Seth's brown eyes brightened at the memory. "She screamed at you and—"

"Chased me through the house! It wasn't my fault though. I followed the directions. I have no idea what went wrong. But, man, did her hair look awful."

"She refused to go to school, remember?" Seth said, barely able to get the words out between laughs. "She made your mom go to the teachers and get her work, and she didn't go to school for like, what?"

"Two weeks. Yeah, that's right. My mom finally took her over to—"

"Deborah Graves—"

"Yep, Mom took her to Deborah's hair salon and had Deborah cut it so short that Amy couldn't even put a hair clip in it."

"Amy kept saying she looked like a boy, and I kept teasing her that wasn't a bad thing because boys were better, and she'd get so mad at me."

"Never for long, though," I said, smiling at the closeness we'd all shared. "My sister adored you. She thought you hung the moon."

More memories bubbled up and out, and as we shared them, in some ways, it seemed like no time had passed at all.

We still finished each other's sentences. We still connected through our sense of humor. We still made each other laugh.

"How's your family?" I asked once we'd thoroughly caught up on mine. "What's everyone up to?"

"Noah's teaching elementary school, if you can imagine my brother doing that. I don't think you ever knew his wife, Karlie, but no loss. Their marriage was short-lived."

Probably not as short-lived as mine, I thought.

He reached into his back pocket and pulled out his phone, scrolling through to show me pictures.

"That's his little boy, Thomas. He's five."

"Oh, how handsome! He looks just like Noah. Spitting image, in fact."

"Yeah, he's a good kid, and Noah's a great dad. He's done an incredible job with that kid, and he's been raising him alone since Thomas was only six months old."

"Six months? Where's his mom?"

"She left."

"Who the hell leaves a six-month-old?"

"Karlie, evidently. She's got...issues. Trust me, Thomas is better off with Noah, and Noah's better off without Karlie."

"And what about your little sister? What kind of trouble is Zara getting into these days?"

"Zara is frickin' awesome. She amazes me. She's got one year left in school, and then she'll be Dr. Zara Donovan, veterinarian."

"What? No way! She can't be old enough for that. Wait—how old is she now?"

"She's twenty-six."

"No! How is that possible? I still see her in my head at thirteen, boy-crazy and giving your mom fits."

"Yeah, well, she's all grown up now. I think being the youngest, Mom's illness hit her the hardest, you know? Noah and I were both out of the house by the time Mom was diagnosed with MS. At first, Zara rebelled against it, as though she could keep it from happening if she caused enough of a ruckus. But then as Mom got sicker, Zara had no choice but to accept it. She straightened out, quit all her shenanigans, and somehow made it through high school. Then, she went on to college and has busted her ass to get where she's at today. I couldn't be more proud of her."

I smiled at the idea of the freckled-face teenager with the long braids being a veterinarian. She'd always loved animals, and every time their mother turned around, Zara had brought home another creature to rescue.

"I'd love to see her," I said, surprised at the warmth that filled my heart with the thought.

"I'm sure she'd love that, too. I'll tell her to look you up the next time she's in town."

His family. My family. At one time, the lines were blurred, and we all belonged to each other. Zara had been just as much my kid sister as she was Seth's, and Amy had been his even more than she was mine.

I'd been closest to his mother, Eileen, but I'd turned my back on her along with everyone else. My heart hurt to think of how I'd betrayed them all.

"How's your mom doing now?" I asked, though the topic was painful for us both. "Amy said she's using an electric scooter?"

"Yeah, she has good days and bad. Some days she can't even get out of bed, but she's still here, fighting. Mentally and emotionally, she's as strong as ever. Her body just can't keep up with her anymore."

My eyes filled with tears as my heart choked in a deluge of regret and guilt. So much lost. So much hurt inflicted. And what had I gained from it?

"Hey, hey, now. It's okay," Seth said as he grabbed a napkin from the dispenser on the table and handed it to me. "They've got her on good meds, and she's doing her physical therapy like a champ. She's been experimenting with different foods and herbal supplements, too. I think some of that's helping. Seems to be, anyway."

"I'm sorry. I didn't mean to get upset."

"You don't have to apologize," Seth said. "I appreciate that you care how she's doing."

His eyes were so tender, his face so familiar. It was both comforting and depressing at the same time.

"I'm so sorry," I said again, the tears flowing faster. "I never meant to hurt you, Seth. I never meant to hurt your family, or my family, for that matter. I was so selfish. I couldn't see beyond what I wanted."

He reached across the table and took my hand in his. "You were young. We both were. Fresh out of college, it's hard to see everyone else's big picture. At that age, you just wanna look through your own lens, you know?"

I turned my hand in his to grip it tightly, not wanting him to let go or pull away.

"I was certain if I left here, if I went to Chicago without you, that you'd follow me. I was so sure of your love that I thought I could use it to force you to do what I wanted. That was wrong of me."

He took in a deep breath as he reached to take my other hand in his, our grips matching in intensity.

"It was never about me not loving you, Dani. My heart belonged to you since the first day I laid eyes on you in that kindergarten class. I came home and told Mom I'd met the girl I was gonna marry. I thought you were my destiny, and when you left town, you took my heart with you. But my family needed me. Mom was getting sicker, even more than I knew at the time because she and Dad hid that from us kids as long as they could. Of course, even they didn't know what was causing it until after you'd gone. Dad had his hands full with Mom and with Zara acting out. I know you and I had made promises, and I never meant to break them. I wanted to leave with you, babe, to just escape. But I couldn't."

"I know. And I knew that then, but I was selfish. We'd been planning to get out of here since we were in middle school, and I'd held onto that for so long, I couldn't let it go."

Feelings long buried rose up inside me, and for the first time ever, I had the courage to spit them out and expose them to the air, to be rid of them.

"I feel horrible admitting this, but I think in some ways, I resented your mother's illness for messing everything up. The way I looked at it then, when I was young and stupid, your mom had your dad and two other kids to take care of her. I figured she didn't need you as much as I did. I had no idea it would turn out to be multiple sclerosis. I didn't have a clue what she would go through. What you *all* would go through. God, talk about self-centered!" I hung my head in shame and tried to pull my hands away, but he held on, refusing to let go.

"Hey, you couldn't have known."

I forced myself to look up, to meet his eyes and take responsibility for what I had done to him. For what I'd done to us.

"I guess I never considered her feelings when it came to you leaving with me. I certainly never considered yours, and what it would mean for you to stay. I'm sorry I wasn't there for you when you needed me most. I wish I could go back—" I looked back down as the tears came again.

He stood and came to sit beside me in the booth, tucking his thumb beneath my chin to bring my eyes back to his as he put his other arm around my shoulders.

"Like I said, we were both young. If I had it to do over again, I'd have driven to Chicago when you stopped taking my calls, and I would have found you and made you come home with me. I would have never let you leave my side. But I felt rejected, and I was just as stubborn as you and just as determined not to give in. We can't go back. It is what it is, and it's all water under a bridge that washed out a long time ago."

I don't know what possessed me to kiss him in that moment. It wasn't something I'd intended to do. I didn't weigh the consequences or consider what it meant. I didn't even really think about. It was purely impulse and raw need, and maybe a little whiskey.

He didn't pull away. He didn't even hesitate. His lips parted the moment I pressed mine against them, and neither of us held back in any measure.

The bar disappeared along with its patrons. The passage of time was gone, along with all the hurts and heartaches that had come with it. Suddenly, the choices of the past held no sway, and it was just me and Seth again.

I'd forgotten the way he could make my body respond. When you unlock all your firsts together, there's no barriers to exploration, and he'd learned long ago what I liked and how I liked it, and somehow, he hadn't forgotten a thing.

A loud comment from a fellow patron walking by brought us back to present reality, and Seth pulled away with a grin.

"Wow," he said, his breathing heavier and his eyes dark with desire. "I must say, that was a much more satisfying apology than the first one."

Having no idea how to respond to what had just transpired, I reached for my whiskey and downed it.

"Damn!" Seth said. "How many does that make for you tonight, D? Three, that I know of. Should I be worried that you're saying and doing things you won't remember in the morning?"

"I remember everything."

And suddenly, I did.

It was like I had pushed Seth and every memory connected to him as far into the recesses of my mind as possible. Long ago, I'd tried to banish him from my thoughts and sworn never to revisit the decision, and yet, here he was, and everything I'd locked away came flooding back in an overwhelming tide.

Why on earth had I been so damned selfish? Why had I been so obnoxiously stubborn? I'd walked away from the best thing I'd ever had in my life, and I'd convinced myself I was better off for having done it.

I'd thrown myself into my work and turned my back on everything and everyone in Cedar Creek, refusing to visit my own family unless there was a funeral, because I was so scared that seeing Seth would remind me of what I'd lost. Of what I'd tossed away.

"You wanna get out of here?" he asked, and I nodded, willing to go anywhere if it meant prolonging this moment with him.

THREE

Seth scooted out of the booth to stand, holding his hand out to help me do the same.

The whiskey buzz combined with emotional euphoria made me dizzy, and I leaned against the table to steady myself as I tightened my grip on his hand.

He put his arm around me and cocked his head to look at me.

"Whoa. You all right?"

"Yeah," I said with a nod. "It just hit me when I stood up; that's all."

"So, maybe you did have a little too much to drink?" He grinned, but disappointment flashed in his eyes.

He probably thought I was only talking to him because I was drunk.

"I'm fine, I swear." I held up my hand in protest, squaring my shoulders to stand straighter.

"I've never known you to drink hard liquor."

"Yeah, you said that before, but I'm sure there's a lot you don't know about me," I said with a grin. "Whiskey happens to be my drink of choice now."

He frowned, his face scrunched in disgust. "Never could stomach the stuff, myself. I'll stick with beer."

"Maybe you've never tried the right whiskey. Have you ever thought about that? Let's go to my place, and I'll show you what you've been missing."

Both his eyebrows shot up, and my cheeks grew hot as I thought about how my words could be interpreted.

"With whiskey, Seth! Get your mind out of the gutter."

Although, truth be told, my mind had already been there since the moment he'd asked if I wanted to leave.

"My mind wasn't..." He bit down on his bottom lip with a grin. "Okay, yeah, maybe it was."

"Just because I kissed you and invited you back to my place? Did you really think I'd make it that easy?"

He shook his head and laughed. "No. I should have known better."

"C'mon, we need to stop by the liquor store on the way. I have a few varieties at home, but there's a couple more I'd like you to try."

"That's not necessary," he said as we walked toward the front door. "I really don't need to taste whiskey again to know I don't like it. Besides, I don't think it's a good idea for you to have more."

I glared over my shoulder at him as we stepped outside onto the sidewalk. "I told you I'm fine. I think I know my own limit by this point in life."

As luck would have it, I stumbled over an uneven seam in the sidewalk as the words left my mouth, and after reaching out to steady me, Seth clamped his mouth shut and lifted both hands, his eyes filled with mirth.

"It was the sidewalk," I said, pointing to the raised area. "I wasn't looking where I was going."

"I didn't say a word. But I think maybe you need to leave your car here and let me drive you home."

"Yeah, well, my car's not here. I'm living in Gran's house, so it's only three blocks. I knew I wouldn't be able to drive home."

His grin faded, and his brow furrowed.

"So, you intended to drink too much before you ever came?"

"Did becoming a deputy make you a boy scout or something? Yeah, I planned to have a few drinks tonight. It's not like an every night thing, okay? Like I told you earlier, I've been going through some stuff. I've had a bad day."

Somehow, I'd managed to forget about Victor and his move to the federal prison as Seth and I talked, but suddenly, reality crashed back into my thoughts, and with it came the memory of Metro Man and the possibility that I was in danger. That I was putting Seth in danger.

I scanned the area for any sign of a skinny killer in flood water pants, but the street appeared deserted other than two groups of smokers hanging out under the street lights in front of the bar and a couple locked in an embrace against the back of a car down by the corner.

"Hey, you okay?" Seth asked, his hand going to my elbow. "What's wrong? What are you looking for?"

"Nothing," I said, meeting his eyes with a shaky smile.

I tried to convince myself again that Metro Man posed no danger. He'd been interested in hooking up, nothing more.

But something in my gut didn't feel right, and I knew I needed to say goodbye to keep Seth safe, just in case.

The streetlights blurred as my eyes glassed over with disappointment. I'd just wanted to escape. I'd wanted to go back in time and experience what might have been, what could have been. But yet again, my mistake with Victor overshadowed everything.

Perhaps it was for the best, though. No need to bring Seth into the mess I'd made of my life, even if only for one night.

"You know what?" I said, blinking back any threat of tears. "You're probably right. I am a little woozy, and it might be best if I just mosey on home. How about a raincheck on the whiskey lesson?"

The creases in his brow deepened, concern evident in his dark eyes.

"Yeah, sure. No problem. I'll drive you, though."

"No, you don't have to do that," I said, taking a step back from him as I did another quick scan of the street. The idea of walking home alone with a possible killer out there frightened me, but the thought of Seth being hurt because of me was even more terrifying. "It's a few blocks. The fresh air will do me good."

"Then, I'll walk with you." He reached to take my hand, but I pulled it from his reach.

"No, that's nonsense. Go back inside. Enjoy your Friday night with your friends. I'll be fine, really."

I hoped that was true.

"I am not about to let you walk home alone drunk. Now, you can either get in my truck, or I'll walk with you. What's it gonna be?"

"Seriously, I walk home from this bar all the time. It's not that far."

"Great, then let's start walking."

He headed in the direction of my grandmother's house, and I scrambled to find a reason to keep him at the bar where I knew he'd be safe.

"But what about your truck? You can't just leave it here."

He turned back to face me, but he didn't stop walking.

"Like you said, it's not that far. I'll just walk back here to get it. C'mon."

Without waiting for my response, he turned and continued on his path.

I growled in frustration and then hurried to catch up with him.

"You are the most stubborn person I've ever met in my life," I said once we were side by side.

"Really? I would think I have some pretty stiff competition from the person you see in the mirror every day."

"Oh, no." I shook my head. "You are way more stubborn than I am."

"Then why waste time arguing with me? Watch your step." He

pointed to a hole in the sidewalk, reaching to put his arm around my waist and steer me clear of it.

"I'm not drunk, I swear."

"Okay. I didn't want you to trip or twist your ankle. That can happen when you're sober, too, you know."

He didn't move his arm from my waist, and we settled into an easy stride, falling in step without any effort from either of us.

It felt so familiar, and yet so foreign. I'd walked by his side the same way more times than I could ever count, but it had been so long. A lifetime ago, it seemed.

The haziness of my whiskey buzz only served to enhance the surreal qualities of being back in Cedar Creek, back in Seth's embrace, and back to a version of myself I thought I'd lost forever.

I didn't want it to end. It felt right being with him. It felt good to laugh again. To be understood. To be known. To feel safe.

It was almost like an alternate universe where I could see how it always should have been, and I wasn't ready to let go of the comfort of that just yet.

But as our journey drew closer to its end, my thoughts were at war.

Part of me wanted to throw caution to the wind in every imaginable way and invite Seth inside to see what other memories we could revisit. But another part of me couldn't shake the nagging feeling that Metro Man was in some way connected to Chicago and the mistakes I'd made there.

"The place looks good," Seth said as we walked up the stone path to the porch of my grandmother's house.

"Thanks, but the credit goes to my cousin Garrett. He moved in here when Gran died, and he spent a nice sum on renovations inside and out. He even gave the house a fresh coat of paint and some updated landscaping just before I moved in."

Seth looked around with an appreciative nod as we climbed the steps to the porch. "Where's Garrett now?"

"He works for a law firm in one of those high-rise buildings in downtown Orlando. He got tired of the commute and moved to a condo overlooking Lake Eola, a few blocks from work."

"I knew I hadn't seen him around town in a while. How's his sister? Gigi?"

"Good, I guess," I said as I pulled the house keys from my purse. "Still living in Hawaii, so life can't be that bad."

"Yeah, she was telling me about island life when I saw her at your grandmother's funeral. Sounds like she loves it there."

"Wait," I said, holding up my hand with a slight shake of my head. "You were at Gran's funeral?"

"Of course. I had to pay my respects. You know I always loved your grandma. I stopped by and checked on her now and then after you left. She was a sweet lady."

My eyebrows scrunched together, and my eyes narrowed as I replayed Gran's funeral in my head, searching the memory reel for any sign of Seth.

"I never saw you," I concluded.

He shrugged. "I didn't think you'd want to. I came in at the last minute and sat in the back, and I left once the service was done."

"You were at my grandmother's funeral, and you didn't even say hello?"

"Dani," he said with a scoffing chuckle, "you hadn't spoken to me in *years*. You'd stopped taking my calls when you left, and everyone I talked to in your family at the time made it clear you didn't want to have anything to do with me. I figured it was a difficult enough time for you to say goodbye to your grandmother. I didn't want to cause any drama or create any tension. I got in, I gave my condolences to several members of the family, and I got out."

My mouth dropped open and then closed again. "No one ever told me you were there."

He shrugged again. "I don't know why. It's not like I asked people not to say anything."

I had wondered if he would show. I'd thought about it the entire flight home from Chicago. It was the first time I'd been back to Cedar

Creek since leaving him, and I'd fretted over what I might say if we came face to face.

I'd told myself that I hoped he wouldn't come, but then when I thought he hadn't, my heart had hurt with disappointment. Now, to think that he had been there all along made me wonder how things might have turned out differently if I had seen him.

After spending time with him tonight, there was no denying the attraction between us was still strong. Would we have rekindled our connection then? Would we have begun talking again? And if so, would that have kept me safe from the destruction Victor brought into my life?

I couldn't imagine that I ever would have fallen for Victor if I'd still had any hope with Seth. Looking back, I could acknowledge that much of the reason I allowed myself to be swept along in Victor's wake was loneliness and a yearning for connection and passion in my life.

If I'd had Seth...I shook my head to dispel the train of thought.

"What? What's wrong?" he asked.

"Nothing. I just can't believe you didn't even say hello."

I unlocked the door and turned back to face him, uncertain of my next move. Should I risk inviting him in? Even without the possibility of a hitman waiting in the shadows, was it safe for either of us to take this further?

Seth hadn't moved from the edge of the porch where he stood at the top of the steps. He didn't seem eager to come inside, and I frowned, disappointed that the decision appeared to have been made for me.

"All right, well, I guess I'll be going," he said, his hands shoved in his pockets. "It was nice seeing you. I appreciate the apologies, and, you know, everything you said before."

I nodded, my heart in my throat. With every fiber of my being, I wanted to invite him to stay. I wanted to be back in his arms, his lips against mine, his hands on my skin, and my body beneath his.

It would likely be a great night, but it was a bad idea, and I struggled to convince myself of that by trying to explain to him.

"I would ask you in, but it's probably not safe."

His eyes widened. "Is that what you think? I know we joked about it, but trust me, I wouldn't make a move on you while you're in this condition. You're perfectly safe."

Shaking my head, I took a step toward him, eager to explain.

"That's not at all what I meant! I would be thrilled for you to make a move on me right now." I frowned when I realized I'd said that out loud. God, I was such an idiot. I was only making things worse. "Forget I said that, please. What I meant was, I have a lot of things going on in my life that are not normal, okay? I made decisions in Chicago that have had long-lasting consequences. Things I can't explain, but believe me when I say, you're better off not involved."

"I understand," he said with a quick nod as he looked away and then back to me. "But hey, tonight was a fun stroll down memory lane. You take care, and I'm sure I'll see you around town. I'm glad we can be friendly now. We can, right?"

Nodding, I opened my mouth to tell him the truth—that I was only trying to look out for him—but I knew that if I explained my fears about Metro Man to Seth, it would only make him want to protect me. It would only serve to get him more entangled. The only way I could truly care for him was to let him walk away.

"Yeah. Of course, we can," I said, even as my heart screamed, *"Ask him in, ask him in."*

My mind tried hard to ignore my heart's pleas, but then he turned and walked down the steps, and I was too selfish to allow him to go. I told myself there was likely no real danger. That I'd been imagining things. That the only real threat I was facing was Seth being gone from my life again.

I'd just gotten him back a couple of hours ago. I wasn't ready to say goodbye yet.

"Wait," I said, and he paused and looked back at me. "You're already here. I might as well go ahead and start your whiskey lesson now. I mean, if you're up for it."

His gaze turned toward the street, and I knew he was likely weighing the same options as me, but with different stakes. He didn't know our lives could be in danger. He only knew I'd hurt him in the past, and I was certain that factored into his decision-making process.

So faint I could barely make out the words, he swore beneath his breath and whispered, "What the hell am I doing?"

Then, he turned back and climbed the steps.

"I suppose I could come in for a few minutes."

And just like that, the decision was made to bring Seth into my complicated, messy life.

FOUR

"Oh! Wow. You're in luck." I was on my knees in front of the small liquor cabinet my cousin had left behind when he moved out. "Garrett has a better whiskey selection than I thought. I hadn't done much digging around in here since I tend to stick to my favorites—oh, what do we have here?" I reached deep into the back of the cabinet and pulled out a bottle of Balvenie Scotch. "Nice!"

I stood and went to retrieve a wooden cutting board from the cabinet next to the stove. "I don't have an official oak board, so you'll have to make do with this for our whiskey flight."

Seth laughed and rubbed his hand across the back of his neck. "You're cracking me up. I'm telling you, I don't like whiskey. You really don't have to go to all this trouble."

"I promised you a whiskey lesson." I pulled shot glasses from the upper shelf of the cabinet by the fridge and then frowned. "Uh-oh. Looks like we're gonna have a mismatched set."

"I didn't stay for the whiskey, okay? I stayed because I enjoy your company, and I wasn't ready to say goodbye yet. Can we maybe just sit and talk?"

"Of course. We can sit and talk while we sample whiskey. Here, take this to the living room." I handed him the cutting board with the glasses stacked on top of it, and I carried as many bottles as I could manage and then made a second trip.

Once I'd gotten everything arranged on the coffee table and poured a sample in each glass, I sat next to Seth on the sofa.

"Is this one Japanese?" he asked as he picked up the Mars Iwai Tradition. "I had no idea Japan made whiskey. Wait, why do they spell it without the '*e*'? That bottle, too." He pointed to the Big Horn Canadian whisky and began to check the other labels.

I shrugged. "I don't really know why, but I think only the United States and Ireland have the '*e*'. I know Scotland, Canada, and Japan spell it without the '*e*', and I haven't drunk from anywhere else really to know."

He tapped the lids on the Old Elk and the Cooper's Craft. "And these are bourbons. U.S. whiskeys, right?"

I grinned, pleased at his interest. "Right. Completely different process for those. The distilleries have to follow very strict procedural guidelines to be classified as a bourbon—like it has to be at least fifty-one percent corn, for instance—and they regulate what kinds of barrels can be used, what proof it can be, and how long it needs to age. I won't bore you with all the specifics though."

Seth grinned. "You're really into this, aren't you?"

I nodded. "Yeah. I am. It started with just enjoying a nice glass of Jameson to relax after work, but then I kept trying new variations and learning more about it, and I guess you can say it fascinates me. The subtle differences in flavors depending on which grain is used, the barrel used, the distilling process. But instead of telling you, let me show you." I picked up the glass with the Cooper's Craft. "Since we're discussing the bourbons, we'll start there. This is a small batch bourbon from Kentucky."

He took the glass to his lips as soon as I handed it to him, and I laid my hand on his arm and pulled it back with a laugh before he could drink.

"Not yet!"

"I thought we were tasting." His forehead wrinkled with confusion.

"We are, but that doesn't mean just turning up your glass and swallowing. I want you to smell it first."

He placed his nose above the glass and inhaled. "Smells like whiskey."

"Okay, but what else do you smell?"

He shrugged. "I smell whiskey."

"All right, all right. Do this. Open your mouth and smell it again with your mouth open."

His eyes widened as he did what I'd instructed. "Wow. That smells different somehow. Almost like tobacco."

"Right? Smell it that way again. Any floral scents? Fruity scents? You might also be picking up a hint of charred wood because of the way Cooper's Craft prepares their barrels. Did you know whiskeys can have over two hundred flavors? That's why you pick up on different notes when you use your senses in different ways. Now, press your left nostril closed and smell again."

His eyes widened more as he gave a slight nod. "Okay, that time I definitely picked up on the floral. That's so bizarre."

"Isn't it? Try the right nostril." I waited for his reaction and then took the bottle and poured a couple of drops in my hand. "Now, pour just a couple of drops from your glass into your hand, and then clap your palms together a few times and rub them briskly, like this."

When he'd followed my example, I lifted my palms to my nose, breathing in the heady scent of corn.

"Do you smell the grain?"

"I'll be damned," Seth said with a grin. "I smell corn."

"Okay, now you can take a sip, but hold it on your tongue and move it around a bit, almost like you're chewing it. It's called a Kentucky chew."

He did as he was told, and then I instructed him to swallow, watching for his reaction, and then laughing as he squinted and whistled.

"And there's the burn," he said in a hoarse voice. "That's why I don't like whiskey."

"Do you feel it here?" I laid my hand across his collarbone and smiled when he nodded. "Ah, see? That's the Kentucky hug! Believe it or not, different whiskeys burn in different ways. Here, try this one."

I lifted the glass with the sample of the Japanese Mars Iwai Tradition and handed it to him.

"Don't forget to smell it first."

"Hmmm," he said as he held his mouth open and breathed it in. "With this one, I smell caramel. And...is that honey?"

I nodded and talked him through the rest of the steps before having him take a sip.

"Where does that one burn?" I asked when he'd swallowed.

He scrunched his nose and shook his head. "It feels like I got water up my nose. How do you drink this stuff and enjoy it?"

Laughter came so easily when I was with him. It took no effort to find it, and I marveled at how alive I felt after being numb for so long.

God, he was so damned handsome. This was the face that had haunted my dreams. The smile that would come to me when I least expected it, the one I pictured whenever I saw anything that reminded me of him. How could thirteen years have passed since I'd seen that smile up close?

It pulled at me like a magnet I could no longer resist.

"You might like it better over ice," I said, leaning in to bring our faces closer together. "As the ice melts, the water allows the other flavors to open up." Closer still. "It kind of mellows out the alcohol and makes it smoother." We were so close I could feel the warmth of his breath, and a shiver of desire rippled through me as his gaze shifted to my mouth. "It's more like velvet on your tongue. Easier to swallow."

My lips trembled as they brushed his, and when his parted in response, I took that as encouragement and went all in, grabbing the back of his head with both hands and pulling him to me so I could better explore.

He shifted his upper body to wrap his arms around me, matching my enthusiasm as the kiss deepened and our tongues intertwined.

I gripped his shoulders as I twisted on the couch to face him, our mouths never parting as I drew my knee up and into his lap. He hugged my leg closer against him and stroked his fingers down the inside of my calf with a touch so featherlight that I shivered. Hell, I think I even moaned a little, which made him chuckle deep in his throat.

The ringing of my cell phone in my pocket startled us both, and I jerked back to pull it out and toss it on the table.

"Do you need to answer that?" he asked as he reached to brush my hair back behind my ear.

"No. They'll call back if it's important."

I leaned forward to return to our kiss, but he shifted his position to sit back against the couch, just out of my reach. He braced his elbow on top of the sofa cushions, propping his head in his hand as he stared at me with such intensity that I felt I was under a magnifying glass. I sat up straight and adjusted my shirt, uncomfortable with the scrutiny of his gaze.

"What? What are you looking at?"

He shrugged with a half-ass smile. "I'm just looking at you. *Really* looking at you. I haven't been able to do that in an awfully long time, and I want to see what's different and what's the same."

"Oh, God, no." I reached for the larger rocks glass on the end of the board, gulped down the sample and then poured a generous serving of the Balvenie. "Your last good look, I was, what? Twenty-two? Thirty-five is a lot different, trust me. I've got the start of wrinkles right here around my eyes, and you'll see that when I smile, the lines around my mouth—the ones they call parentheses—they're still there when I stop smiling. Faint, for now, but it won't be long before they're visible all the time. You'll probably also notice this line right here between my eyebrows." I pointed for emphasis. "That's been a recent development. Oh, and I noticed another gray hair has popped up in my part. I pull them out with an angry vengeance when I find them, but they keep coming back. It's to be expected, I suppose, since my mother started going gray in her late twenties, but damn, it's depressing."

I took another drink as he continued to scrutinize me, and he reached for my glass and set it on the table. Then, he took my hand in his and brought it to his lips.

"I don't see any of that. I see the same girl I've always seen. A little older, a little more worldly, perhaps. But still just as beautiful as she's always been."

A warm blush crept into my cheeks, and I pulled my hand away and ran my fingers through my hair.

"So, back to the whiskey flight." I took a deep breath and vowed to avoid eye contact so I wouldn't get lost in his eyes again. "We haven't done a Canadian one yet. The rye makes it quite peppery."

"Look, I appreciate the lesson, and I admire that it's obviously something you're passionate about. But can we just talk? Why did you decide to move back to Cedar Creek?"

I considered telling him the truth. Spilling my guts and emptying it all out.

After all, for most of my life, he'd been my best friend. My confidante. He'd understood me better than anyone ever had. He'd known me, inside and out, and if there was anyone I could trust other than my immediate family, I knew it was Seth.

But I also knew that the more people I talked to about Victor, the more I risked putting them in danger. I had no way of knowing what the Mafia might do. How they might retaliate against Victor if he chose to testify and tell what he knew. How they might use me, or those closest to me, as some kind of bargaining chip to keep his silence.

Of course, in order for that to be effective, I would need to be someone Victor held dear. Who knew how he really felt about me?

Our entire relationship had been built on lies. He might have never loved me at all.

I shoved away thoughts of Victor and the shame that came with them. I shoved away caution and reason. I shoved away everything in my mind except one thought. Escape.

Grabbing the glass from where Seth had set it, I took one quick swig to empty it, and then before he could react, I moved to straddle Seth's lap. I bent to kiss him, desperate to feel anything other than confusion, betrayal, regret, and fear.

His body responded without question at first, his mouth opening to welcome me again as he ran his hands up my back and twisted them into my hair. For a few blissful seconds, passion led the way, the physical overpowering the mental and emotional as we allowed our bodies to do as they wished.

This kiss was primal and raw, more urgent and demanding than before. Desires long held in check broke free, and the passion we'd shared in our youth was once again unleashed. I arched forward to press myself against him, and he tore his lips from mine to bury his face in my neck, his mouth greedy on my skin as he brought his hands around to cup my breasts.

The barriers of time fell away in our haste to reconnect and reclaim, and as my hips rocked against his, I reached between us and undid his belt.

Immediately, his hand closed over mine, and he pulled back with a swearing growl. He moved his hands to my hips, stilling them as he lay his head back against the sofa cushion and looked up at me, his eyes wild with desire and his breath unsteady.

"What's wrong?" I asked.

"Dani, I—" He groaned with another swear.

"What?" I lay my hands on his chest, my eyes searching his. "What's wrong?"

He shook his head and rubbed his hand across his brow. "I can't do this."

Disappointment washed over me, followed by rejection, which I was in no condition to take.

"Why? Is there someone else? Are you seeing someone?"

I had no evidence at all to suggest that. It was a straw my mind pulled, an effort to have there be an explanation that wasn't about me.

"No," he said with a frown. "I wouldn't be here at all if I were seeing someone else. There isn't anyone."

So, it *was* rejection. And it stung more than I could have ever imagined.

When he didn't follow me to Chicago, it had nearly killed me. I'd been so sure of his love, so certain he'd follow if I left, and when he refused to, it devastated me. The only way to survive had been to convince myself I didn't need him. That I didn't need anyone.

Loving other people gave them power over your life and your decisions. I'd sworn to never do that again, and until Victor, I'd kept that promise to myself.

But buried deep beneath all that bravado, I'd carried a flicker of hope. I'd kept it hidden away in my heart, protected even from my own mind, lest I extinguish it and cause it to die.

That hope had been simple. Seth loved me. I knew he did. If his refusal to come away with me was because of family obligations, nothing more, than that meant if I ever returned to Cedar Creek, he'd take me back.

What if I'd been wrong?

I moved to raise myself from his lap, and his hands gripped my hips tighter, holding me in place as he spoke.

"Wait. Listen to me, please. I can see the hurt in your eyes, and that's not my intent, believe me."

"No, it's fine," I lied, but the buzz of the alcohol combined with the overwhelming pain of his rejection was too much to hide, and my eyes betrayed me with tears. "I shouldn't have come on to you like that."

Swiping at my tears with the back of my hand, I tried again to get up, but he held me firm.

"Please don't cry." He moved one hand to cup my face, his thumb wiping away an errant tear. "God, Dani, it's not that I don't want you. I do. I want to make love to you right now like I have never wanted anyone in my life. It's taking every bit of strength I have to hit the brakes. But if and when we ever...go *there* again, I don't want it to be because you've had too much to drink or you've had a bad day. I want it to be for all the right reasons, and tonight isn't that night."

My phone rang again, and I rolled from him without any resistance on his part.

With another swipe at my tears, I grabbed the phone, frowning to see it was an unknown caller from an Illinois number.

I stared at it as it rang, and Seth leaned forward.

"Aren't you gonna answer it?"

"I don't know. It's probably a telemarketer," I said, though my gut instinct wasn't that at all.

"I can't imagine a telemarketer would call this late at night on a Friday. It might be important." He braced his elbows on his knees as he clasped his hands together. "They've called twice, whoever it is."

I swiped my finger to catch the call before the last ring ended.

"Hello," I said, hoping that curiosity wouldn't kill the cat.

"God, it's good to hear your voice, sweetness," Victor said. "You come to me every night in my dreams, and I wake with that voice in my head. That little touch of a drawl that drives me mad."

It was as if the blood stopped flowing in my veins and the air left my lungs. My entire body trembled in shock, my hand shaking so hard I nearly dropped the phone.

"How did you get this number?" My voice was a hollow croak, barely recognizable.

My obvious distress had alerted Seth that all was not well, and he moved closer immediately, his dark eyes clouded with concern.

I motioned for him to be silent and stood to walk away from him, fighting to keep my knees from buckling beneath me as Victor continued.

"There's no time to explain. I'll tell you when I see you. Right now, I need you to get out of that house as soon as possible. Just go."

My mind moved like it was filled with molasses. How was Victor calling me? How did he get my number? Had he just said he'd see me? How? Why wasn't he in prison? Had they released him? Why wasn't I told? This was ridiculous. I wasn't going anywhere for him.

"I don't want to see you." I forced my voice to remain calm despite the wild panic wreaking havoc inside me. "Don't call this number again."

Seth had stood and come to my side, and I closed my eyes to block him out so I could concentrate on what Victor was saying.

"I understand you're upset with me. You have every right to be. I screwed up. I screwed us up. I can't tell you how much I regret that, and I will spend the rest of our lives making it up to you. But right now, I need you to listen to me, sweetness. Your life is in danger. There are people in Cedar Creek with the intention of doing you harm to get back at me. They've been watching you. Unfortunately, our situation escalated tonight, and they plan to make a move."

I struggled to comprehend what he was saying, my head still fuzzy from the alcohol and reeling at Victor's intrusion.

"What? What are you talking about?"

"I hate that I've brought this on you, but there's very little I can do about it at present. I can't get to you in time to stop them, so I need you to run. You have to leave. Now!" His voice had become more urgent. "Get out of that house and get out of that town. Don't take time to pack. Don't tell anyone where you're going. Just get in the car and drive north. Don't stop for any reason. I'll call you in an hour with more instructions. Do you understand?"

My eyes fluttered open to see Seth staring at me intently. He mouthed something, but I turned away from him, unable to focus on even one conversation, much less two.

"No, I don't understand." I ground out to Victor through gritted teeth. "How dare you put me in this position!"

"I know, I know. But we'll have to discuss all that later. We've already wasted too much time. Tell me you're leaving. Tell me you're headed to the car now."

"I don't—"

"Damn it, Danielle, get in the car and start driving." His pleading turned harsh, his voice frantic. He was shouting, and he'd never once raised his voice at me before. "I know you probably don't trust anything I tell you at this point, but I swear on my life this is the truth. You're in danger, sweetness, and I need you to get the hell out of there."

I definitely didn't trust him, but after everything I'd learned about his life since his arrest, I had no problem believing he had associates who would kill me in retaliation for something he'd done. It was one of the reasons I'd left my life in Chicago behind.

I couldn't think. I couldn't process. I laid my shaking hand across my forehead and tried to force my thoughts to calm.

"I can't just leave," I said, unable to imagine that scenario. "My family, I—"

"Your family will be in danger if you don't go. They'll be in danger if you make any contact with them at all! I'm trying to protect you and protect them, but you gotta do what I say. I need you to listen to me, okay? These people have been watching you for a while now. They've likely been inside your house, and I have no way of knowing what they might have put in place, so you need to get out of there. You can't tell anyone you're leaving. Not your family, not the police, no one. If you do, they'll know and they'll retaliate harder. These are brutal people, and there's no limit to what they'll do."

The shock of hearing Victor's voice had begun to ebb, and as it did, the reality of his words began to sink in. My life was in danger. My family was in danger. The bogeyman I'd feared was real, and he was nearby, ready to kill me. The very house I stood in might blow up at any moment. I had to get out.

"Okay. All right. I'll leave."

"Good. Just drive north. I gotta go for now, but I'll call you in an hour."

"No. Don't call me at all. I'll go because you've put my life in danger, but I don't ever want to talk you again."

"Sweetness, I—"

I ended the call and turned the phone off as Seth exploded with questions.

FIVE

"What's going on? Who was that? What do you mean your life is in danger?"

I pressed my fingers to my temples and tried to think. Victor had said I had no time to pack. He'd made it sound like the threat was imminent. Where was I to go? How long would I need to stay gone? How would I know my family was safe? Couldn't I at least tell them that I was going somewhere without telling them why?

"Dani, talk to me." Seth grabbed my arms and brought my focus back to him. "What's going on? You're white as a ghost and you're shaking all over. Who was that?"

"I have to go."

"Go where?"

I pulled myself from his grasp and turned left and right as I looked around my living room. What should I take with me? How much time did I have? Was someone outside the house now, watching and waiting for me to emerge? Would I be shot down as I pulled the car out of the driveway?

"Would you please just tell me what's going on?" Seth asked, and the realization that he was in danger because of me dawned fast and hard.

"Oh, God, Seth! You have to go. You have to leave. You have to get out of here."

"What? No. I'm not going anywhere. What's going on? Why is your life in danger?"

"Because I'm an idiot who made bad choices and rushed into things. I can't explain it right now. Hell, I don't know that I can ever explain it, but believe me when I say you've got to go. You've got to get as far away from me as possible. Please, leave now before something happens to you because of me."

"I'm not leaving you like this. Tell me what's going on and I can help you. I'll call for backup. I can have this house surrounded in minutes."

"No. Then more people will get hurt, and it will be my fault. I have to leave. You have to leave, too."

I grabbed my purse from the kitchen counter and shoved my phone inside it, and then I grabbed a photo of my family from the living room wall. It was impossible to know what else to take. I had no idea what might happen, what the outcome would be.

"Damn it, Dani. Talk to me. Let me help you."

"You can't, okay? I have to go. Now."

"Go where?" He flung his arms out in frustration. "You're in no shape to drive. You've been drinking all night, and that phone call obviously upset you. Where do you need to go? I'll take you."

"No!" I shouted, and he rocked back on his heels at the vehemence in my voice, his eyes wide with shock. "I'm sorry, Seth. I wish I could explain, but I can't. Please just go. Get away from me so nothing happens to you."

I tried to push past him to head toward the door, and he stopped me, placing his hands on my shoulders.

"I am not letting you drive like this. If you need to go somewhere, I'll take you, but you have to tell me what's going on. Let me help you."

"No," I whispered, my voice cracking under the weight of fear and panic. "You need to get as far away from me as possible."

"Yeah, well, I'm not doing that. I'm not leaving your side until I know that you're okay, and right now, you're pretty freaking far from okay."

"Seth, I don't have time to argue with you. There may be someone waiting outside right now, and I can't say for sure what will happen when we step out there."

He looked toward the windows, and his hand went to his hip where his gun would normally be. "You think someone's outside? Let me call it in."

"No. There's no time. I have to go now."

"Then I'm coming with you."

I laid my hand on my chest in an attempt to ease the wild thumping of my heart.

"If you want to help me, then protect my family. Make sure they're all right. Make sure no one harms them. Let them know I'll contact them as soon as I can."

"I'll make a call and have someone watch over them, but there's no way in hell you're leaving here without me."

I recognized the set of his jaw and the stubborn glint in his eyes, and I knew his mind was made up.

Tears began to stream down my face as I shook my head.

"Don't do this. You can't protect me, and I won't get you killed because of my stupidity. Please, Seth, just go."

I wrapped my arms around his neck and squeezed him tighter than I ever had, and then I pressed my lips against his. The fear coursing through my veins didn't stop the longing for what might have been, and I had to consider that this could be the last time I would ever see Seth. If I didn't make it out alive, or if I couldn't come back to Cedar Creek, I'd never have another chance to kiss him. To tell him what I needed him to know.

I held his face in my hands as I pulled back from the kiss and gazed into his eyes, dark with fear and confusion.

"I love you, Seth," I whispered. "I've always loved you—always. And I always will. But I'm begging you, if you've ever cared for me at all, let me walk away. Don't try to go with me. I need you here in Cedar Creek with my family, okay?"

"No. Let me call for help." His voice rose as I shook my head and tried to pull away from his grasp. "Listen to me. Are you forgetting I'm a deputy sheriff? I have an entire team of people I can call. They can be here in minutes."

"No!" I screamed. "For all I know, this house might have been rigged with explosives. We have to get out of here now."

"Explosives?" He released my shoulders as his face registered the shock of my words. "What the hell are you talking about?"

"For God's sake, would you listen to me? We have to go."

"Okay," he said, finally moving toward the door with a sense of urgency. "Let's go to the station. It's only a few blocks away."

"No. We can't do that."

I didn't doubt the capabilities of Cedar Creek's local law enforcement, but this was the Mafia we were talking about. The Chicago Outfit. The Empire. One of the most dangerous and most powerful mob families in the country. A police presence wouldn't exactly scare them off, and I shuddered to think what might happen if it came to a standoff. I didn't want to be responsible for innocent lives lost.

Besides that, who knew what kind of contacts they might have working with them, even here? I'd learned from the federal prosecutors who questioned me in Chicago that there were members of law enforcement all over the place who were on the Mafia's payroll, and they'd cautioned me to be wary of who I talked to and what information I gave about Victor.

It seemed farfetched that anyone in Cedar Creek's force would be tainted, but I couldn't know for sure, and I couldn't risk Seth's life or the lives of his fellow officers because of my naivety in trusting the wrong man to marry.

It was best for me to be the only target. That might be the only way I could save the people I loved.

I reached for the doorknob, but Seth grabbed it first, moving me behind him.

He bent to pull a pistol from his ankle holster, and then he looked over his shoulder at me. "Is your car unlocked?"

I pressed the unlock button on the key fob. "It is now."

"Stay behind me. We're going down the steps and to the car. You get in the driver's seat and climb across, and I'm getting in behind you."

I opened my mouth to protest him getting in the car with me, but fear at the thought of what we faced on the other side of the door overruled my objection, and I clamped my mouth shut. I took one look back at my peaceful little abode and hoped I'd see it again. My gaze landed on the whiskey bottles lined up on the coffee table, and I sprinted to grab the Jameson.

"What are you doing?" Seth asked.

"Grabbing essentials. Okay, let's go."

He took the keys from me and crouched low as he opened the door leading out to the carport. I held my breath while we scurried down the steps and alongside the car, and then I dove inside while he held the driver's door open. The shifter stick shoved into my ribs as I made my way to the passenger seat, and I bit down hard on my lip and tried not to cry out.

"Stay down," Seth said as he slid into the driver's seat, his eyes darting to the rearview mirror and side mirrors as he put the key in the ignition.

A terrifying thought came to me, and I grabbed his arm and pulled it back in a panic. "What if the car is rigged to explode? In the movies, they turn the key and the bomb goes off. How would we know?"

"Jesus! Who did you piss off, and what are you involved in?"

"I told you, it's a long story. But is there a way to know if the car is safe?"

"I wish to hell I had my truck, and I wish I knew what I was up against."

He put his hand back on the key and paused, his eyes meeting mine as he turned it slowly.

We both released held breaths as the engine roared to life, and then he instructed me to get down as low as possible as he began to back out of the carport.

"We're supposed to go north," I said without even considering why.

"We're going to the station."

"What? I told you we can't do that."

"Why not? That's the safest place for us to be."

I shook my head. "No, it's not, and if I go to the police now, and they see me do that, then my family is only going to be in more danger."

"I'll call ahead," he said, pulling his phone from his pocket. "I'll tell them to send patrolmen to your sister's house and your parents' house. But you have to tell me why. I have to know who we're running from."

I reached to take his phone from him. "You can't involve law enforcement, okay? Trust me on this. I've been flying under the radar for the last two years by not doing anything to provoke either side. I can't tell what I don't know, and I can't make it look like I've got anything to tell."

"What the hell are you talking about?" he said, slamming his hand against the steering wheel. "For God's sake, tell me *something*. I'm fighting blindfolded here."

I took as deep of a breath as I could manage in my hunched over position and exhaled with a swear.

"All right, I'll tell you what you want to know, but you have to promise me that you'll keep driving. That you won't go to the station."

"That's ridiculous! Why would I not go to the one place I know I can keep you safe?"

"Because we can't risk getting your fellow officers killed because of me."

He paused his constant surveillance of our surroundings to look down at me. "This threat is that big?"

I nodded. "Yeah. It is."

"I can't believe I'm agreeing to this," he whispered as he went back to scanning for danger in all directions. "No one else on earth could make me go against every instinct I have."

"I'm sorry. I never should have walked up to you in that bar tonight. I never should have asked you back to my place. I shouldn't have involved you. I'm so sorry."

He frowned as he reached over to rub his hand across my back. "It's okay. I wouldn't want you in danger alone. You said head north? Why? Where are we going?"

"I don't know." I replayed Victor's words in my head. He'd wanted me to go north to meet up with him, something I wasn't about to do. "Don't go north. Go, um, west, I guess. Or maybe east?"

"You don't know where we're going? Geez. I thought you had some sort of plan."

"For right now, just drive and let me think." I laid my forehead against the dashboard and closed my eyes.

"As soon as we leave town, we're more vulnerable. As you well know, there's nothing but rural roads heading out of Cedar Creek."

"The back roads are to our advantage here. You know these roads. They don't. Just keep a lookout for anyone following us." I sat up and looked out the rear window, relieved to see no one.

"Who's *they*? Can you at least tell me who we're running from?"

I ignored his question as my mind scrambled to think of a destination. Some place we could be safe long enough for me to catch my breath and think. I needed to think. I needed to calm my thoughts and figure out what to do next. I needed to process everything that had happened since my phone rang.

"Where could we go to lie low and be safe?" I asked, unable to come up with a good option.

"Um, the station would have been a great place, but we're driving away from it because you insisted we had to. You said you'd tell me everything if I did that. So, start talking. Who are we running from?"

"The Mafia."

"The—" He looked over at me, both eyebrows raised and his mouth gaping open. "Seriously?"

"Yeah. The Chicago Outfit. That Mafia."

"Holy shit, D. How'd you get mixed up with them?"

"I'm *not* mixed up with them. My ex is."

He shot a sideways glance toward me. "You married a guy in the Mafia?"

"I didn't know he was in the Mafia when I married him, okay? Where are you going? Why are you turning here? We need to head out of town."

"We also need to make a few detours so that if anyone is following us, I can see who they are." His grip on the steering wheel tightened. "How did you find out he was in the Mafia?"

I laid my head against the passenger window, my mind resistant to the memories recalled by the question.

"He was making breakfast one Saturday morning, and a team of men dressed in black suddenly shattered my windows and burst through my doors. They handcuffed him and carried him away, and I called our attorney, certain that some horrific mistake had been made. But no. I had married a Mafia hitman."

"That must have been terrifying for you," Seth said, reaching over to take my hand. "I can't imagine you going through that."

I lifted my head to look at him, surprised at his reaction, though I shouldn't have been. He'd thought of me and how the situation affected me. By contrast, the others closest to me whom I had told— my parents and my sister—had all expressed outrage first at what a monster Victor was and then condemnation for me at making such a horrible choice in a mate and rushing into such an important life decision.

"Yeah, it definitely wasn't an experience I ever want to repeat. After that morning's rude awakening, I lost myself, financially and emotionally. In the midst of that, I struggled to prove to the court that I didn't know anything—and I honestly didn't—and I struggled to accept everything I learned from them about the man I thought I loved."

He squeezed my hand and released it to resume his grip on the steering wheel, and his sudden tension alerted me to the headlights behind us.

After detouring in a zigzag pattern out of town, we were on a remote stretch of winding rural road with no houses or streetlights visible either in front of or behind us. Towering trees formed a thick barrier on either side of the road, caging us in and leaving us vulnerable, exactly as Seth had predicted.

"Do you think that's someone following us?" I asked Seth as I turned in my seat to look back.

"Hard to tell just yet."

He hit the accelerator as he watched the headlights come closer in the rearview mirror.

I turned to look back again. "They're gaining on us. Do you think we can outrun them?"

"Turn around and get low. Stay down, okay?"

Obeying his instruction, I crouched low and then turned my head so I could watch the lights grow larger in the side mirror.

My heart pounded, and my stomach churned with fear.

We were going so fast that the trees outside the window were a dark blur, and if I hadn't been so worried about the possibility of bullets flying, I might have fretted over the dangers of such high speeds on the curving, narrow road.

The headlights were close enough now to determine that it was a truck, and as it approached us, it began to ride in the middle of the road.

I turned to look at Seth, his face a mask of concentration as he watched the threat behind us while keeping focused on the road ahead as well. His pistol lay on the seat between his legs, and I hoped he wouldn't need to take his hands off the wheel to grab it.

Suddenly, loud muffler pipes roared as the truck gunned the gas to pull alongside us in the left lane, and I held my breath as I watched it, terrified that at any minute, we'd be rammed off the road or gunned down and left to die.

"Hold on," Seth said, and then he hit the brakes hard, screeching us to a halt as the truck kept going.

Despite the danger, I couldn't help looking up and over the dash at the red taillights growing smaller as the distance between us grew.

Seth exhaled, and I gulped in air after holding my breath far too long.

His body was still tense, and his gaze still steely, and something told me not to relax.

"They weren't after us, right?" I asked, looking for reassurance. "We're safe for now, right?"

"That remains to be seen. They could have gotten ahead of us to block the road and fence us in from behind with another car."

"Great. So, what do we do?"

He turned the car around in the middle of the road and accelerated us in the opposite direction.

"We proceed with caution, and we call and get someone to check on your family."

SIX

Something in his demeanor had changed with the knowledge it was likely the Chicago Outfit pursuing us, and it only served to make me even more scared.

"Where's my phone?" he asked, and I was surprised to see it still in my hand. I'd forgotten I took it from him.

"Do you have a partner?" I asked as I handed it to him. "Someone you trust implicitly? The feds warned me that I have to be careful who I involve, and Victor told me outright these people would be watching to see if I went to the cops."

"I'll call Tristan. He's more than a partner; he's like a brother to me. I trust him to keep a low profile and not draw attention to himself."

"What will you tell him?"

He didn't answer me, and I looked down at the family photo in my lap as he made the call to tell Tristan he was in the middle of something he couldn't explain yet and ask him to do a drive by with my parents and my sister.

He had just ended the call when he suddenly slowed the car.

"What are you doing?" I asked as he stopped and shut off the lights.

He put the car in reverse and twisted in the seat so he could see behind us as he backed off the road into a narrow logging lane, unmarked and barely visible in the dark.

"What are you doing?" I repeated. "Where are we going?"

I looked left and right as we backed farther into the logging lane, unable to see anything but trees on either side.

"We're gonna sit still for a minute and see if anyone looks for us."

"What do you mean? Won't we be trapped?"

"Not any more so than we could be on the road."

My eyes began to adjust to the dark, but it didn't make our surroundings any less spooky. I'd thought it was frightening to be moving and feel hunted, but it was nothing compared to sitting still with that same feeling.

I reached for the bottle of whiskey between my feet and turned it up to chug a swig.

"You want some?" I asked Seth before replacing the cap.

"No. Thanks. You know you're not supposed to have an open container of alcohol in the car, right?"

Rolling my eyes with a groan, I set the bottle back on the floorboard. "What are you gonna do, arrest me?"

He smiled and went back to scanning left and right for any sign of headlights.

"So, it was your ex-husband who called you earlier?"

"Yeah. Victor."

His brows scrunched together as he turned to face me. "He's not in jail? Is he out on bond?"

"He's supposed to be in jail. In fact, he was supposed to be transferred to a federal prison earlier today. His initial charges were state crimes. It was only recently he got charged by the feds under the RICO organized crime umbrella."

"But, if he's in a federal prison—"

"Well, that's the thing. I don't think he is. The more I think about it, the more certain I am he's no longer in custody. They're supposed to alert me every time he's moved. They always have, whether it was for a hearing, for a meeting, whatever. I got an alert earlier today about the move to the federal prison, but nothing since then. If he was released for some reason, no one let me know. But then again, wouldn't they let me know if he escaped?"

"They'll be looking for him if he escaped. That should be easy to find out." He lifted his phone and moved his fingers across the screen, and then he swore and laid it on his leg. "I need to get out from under these trees and get closer to civilization to reach the internet. Tell me exactly what this guy said to you on the phone."

I struggled to recall a conversation I'd been trying hard to forget.

"Victor said I was in danger, and that there were people in Cedar Creek who wanted to harm me to get back at him."

"Did he tell you there were explosives?"

"No, not specifically. He said they'd been inside my house, and he didn't know what they had put in place. I just, uh, I guess that's how I took it."

"What else did he say?"

"That the situation had escalated tonight, and these people decided to make a move. He said he couldn't get to me in time to stop them, and that I needed to drive north and wait for him to call in an hour."

Seth looked at his watch and frowned. "Does your phone have a strong signal?"

"I don't know. I turned it off."

"Turn it back on, and we'll get you somewhere with a better signal."

"Why? I'm not taking his call. I don't want to talk to him again."

"I understand that, but right now, he's the only source of information we have. He's likely to know if you're still in danger. Why did he want you to drive north? Did he tell you where you were going?"

"No. He said to drive north and not to stop for any reason and not to tell anyone. He said he'd explain everything when he saw me, so that's another reason I think he's out."

Seth swore quietly, and then he looked at me, his expression impossible to read in the darkness.

"Is that what you want to do? Go and see him?"

"No, absolutely not. I meant what I said to you and to him. I don't ever want to talk to Victor again."

"Are you sure? You were adamant that I shouldn't come with you. If I wasn't here now, would you be headed to meet him?"

"No! What the hell? The guy is a murderer, Seth. He killed people and just considered it part of his job. How can you even think I'd be willing to go to him after that?"

"I don't know. You married the guy. You must have loved him at some point for some reason. People do crazy things for love."

He shrugged and gestured with his hands as though to indicate his present situation was an example.

"Yeah, well, I didn't know he was a murderer when I married him. It wasn't something he mentioned when we talked backgrounds and hobbies, okay?"

"What did you think his job was?"

"When I met him, he was at my house to give me an estimate for renovations. As far as I knew, he worked for his uncle's construction company. I had no reason to doubt him."

"And nothing he did made you suspicious? The people he hung around? The weapons he carried?"

"I never saw weapons. I didn't hang out with his associates or whatever they're called. Look, I've already answered all these questions for more attorneys than I can count and more law enforcement officers than I ever thought I'd talk to in my life, not to mention a thorough grilling from my parents and my sister. I didn't know what Victor did, okay? I worked nights at the news station while he did God only knows what, and during the day, it wasn't like I drove around to make sure he was at a construction site. I had no reason not to trust him, so I did."

"It's just hard to believe you never saw anything unusual. I mean, you were a reporter. You're an inquisitive person by nature. Nothing set off your radar for bullshit, eh?"

I laid my head back against the headrest. "Honestly, I wasn't around him all that much. Like I said, we worked opposite shifts, and even on the weekends, one of us usually had work stuff to do. At the time, I thought it was part of what we had in common. We were both workaholics dedicated to our jobs. Little did I know."

"If they're bringing him up on federal charges and he's got people on the outside watching you to keep him in line, he must have been pretty deeply connected."

"Yeah, I guess. My assets have been frozen by the feds, and my attorney says it's all part of a push to get Victor to turn on people higher up than him."

"You're divorced, though, right?"

"Yeah, but it doesn't matter. We were married at the time of his arrest, so that tangled up all our finances, even though his name was on nothing of mine and my name was on nothing of his. It's all so surreal. We were only married for two months. So, two months of my life has overshadowed the last two years of my life."

"Two months? Really?"

I groaned and picked up the whiskey again, wanting to escape the topic however possible. "Yeah. Technically, it was longer since the divorce got held up with the whole arrest and trial thing. But yeah. We lived in the same house for two months. Well, two months and two weeks." I took a swallow and scrunched my face at the burn of the fiery liquid at room temperature. "Gah, I need ice."

"Yeah, well, you also need gasoline."

He dropped the shifter into drive and pulled forward, and my mind went back to high alert.

I'd been so consumed with dredging up the past that I'd forgotten the present and its inherent danger.

"Where are we going? Is it safe?"

"There's been no traffic while we sat here. No one came back to look for us. They might be waiting for us, but either way, we have to get fuel."

"You're not going back to Cedar Creek, are you?"

"No. I'll head toward Groveland. We should have enough gas to make it there. You really should keep at least a half a tank in your car at all times."

"Just in case I get a phone call to tell me I'm being chased by the Mafia?"

"Yeah, among other reasons."

We rode in silence, both of us still tense and constantly on the lookout for any sign we weren't alone.

"I'm sorry that happened to you," Seth said after a while. "I know you must have loved the guy if you married him, and that's a hell of a way to find out someone isn't who you think they are."

"I thought it was love at the time, but looking back, I think maybe I was just lonely. Work was my life, and that was purposeful. It was what I'd intended, and I enjoyed it. But when Victor came into the picture, it was like suddenly there was a world outside the station that I wanted to be part of. I got caught up in the whirlwind, you know?"

Strangely, it didn't feel awkward to discuss my feelings for another man with Seth. He'd always been my best friend, even before he became my crush and my lover. He'd always understood me in ways my parents, my sister, and my closest female friends never had. It seemed natural to pour my heart out to him.

"I should have taken things more slowly. I should have gotten to know Victor better. In hindsight, maybe there would have been warning signs if I'd taken the time to look for them instead of being in such a rush."

"How long did you guys date before you got married?"

"You don't wanna know," I said, my cheeks growing hot in the dark. It was one thing to talk to him about falling in love. It was another to admit how foolish I'd been.

"You don't have to tell me if you don't want to," he said. "You don't have to tell me anything. It's not like you owe me any explanations. Or anyone, for that matter. It's your life, your decisions."

I scoffed and turned to look out the window at the blur of trees. "Tell my parents that. You would think it was me who had murdered people based on their reaction. Of course, they were against it from the start, before we even knew what Victor had done."

"Your parents didn't like him?"

"My parents never met him," I said, looking back to Seth.

His eyes widened in surprise. "Wow. I knew I'd never heard from anyone about you bringing the guy home, but I assumed your mom and dad must have gone to Chicago to meet him instead."

"No."

"Not even for the wedding?"

"The *wedding*" —I made air quotes with my fingers—"was Victor and me standing in front of a county clerk at the courthouse."

"Oh." He looked up at the rear-view mirror and stole a glance at me. "What happened between you and your family after you left? You guys were always close, and then you went away and, like, never came back."

"I couldn't," I said, tracing my fingers across the family photo that lay in my lap.

"What do you mean you couldn't? You couldn't come visit? Why?"

How funny that I could discuss meeting and marrying another man without any awkwardness, but this topic? Much more uncomfortable.

I ran my fingers through my hair and twisted it into a loose bun on my head, pulling a hair elastic from its usual spot around the gear shifter to hold it in place.

"Those first couple of years, I was so damned homesick. I wanted to move back so bad, but I was determined to win. I was determined to show all of you that I could make it there. I worried that if I came back to Cedar Creek—if I saw you or saw them—then I'd give up and move back home. I couldn't risk that. I didn't want to fail at being an adult."

"It wouldn't have been failing to come back and visit your family. Hell, it wouldn't have been failing to move back, if that's what you wanted. No one said you had to make it in Chicago to be a success except you."

"I know that now. But back then, I felt like I had something to prove. That I didn't need you or them. Or Cedar Creek. I didn't want to need anyone because needing them gives them power over you. I refused to let anyone else have the ability to affect what I did or how I did it. I threw myself into work, and eventually, it just became my life, and coming back home wasn't even a consideration because I was too busy and there was no time. I didn't date. I didn't even think about dating really. My life was my work, and I was happy being unattached and on my own."

"Until you met Victor."

I closed my eyes against all the pain that had come with meeting Victor.

"Yep. I made one stupid choice, and now here I am. Back home in Cedar Creek. Broke. No career to speak of as I try to get this theater off the ground with all its barriers and obstacles. I see the disappointment in my parents' eyes every time I'm with them. And I don't blame them."

"I've heard you say a couple of times now that it was stupidity, or a stupid choice. You're not a stupid woman. You made a decision with your heart, and that's not stupid. Our hearts can be foolish, yes, but any time you make a choice to love, you're taking a risk. So, you might have made a risky choice, but I don't think you should say you made a stupid one."

I turned to stare at him, wanting to agree but unable to.

"Seth, Victor moved in the day after I met him, and we got married two weeks to the day later. He turned out to be a Mafia hitman who had murdered people, among his various other crimes. I'd say that was a pretty stupid decision on my part."

Seth's eyebrows shot up, and he covered his mouth with his hand and then made like he was rubbing his chin to hide his reaction.

"Yeah, see?" I crossed my arms and slammed my head back against the seat rest. "Stupidity. I told you."

"You thought you loved the guy, right? It must have seemed like the right decision at the time."

"I appreciate you trying to make me feel better, but there's no getting around how dumb I was, and you don't have to pretend you're not shocked that I would do such a thing. It's shocking, I know."

"Actually, it's not that shocking."

I lifted my head and tilted it to look at him. "What?"

"For someone else, yeah, maybe, but knowing what I do about you, I don't find it shocking at all. You were the first person to jump off the swinging bridge when our church youth group did that mission trip in Panama. When my brother Noah got that dirt bike, you jumped on and took off driving even though you'd never been on one."

"Yeah, and I crashed in your mother's rose bed because I didn't know where the brakes were. Stupidity."

"No, you're looking at it all wrong. You take risks no one else would take. I can think of so many stories of you doing that when we were growing up. When it's something you want or something that intrigues you, you dive right in. You don't take time to weigh all the consequences or think about everything that could go wrong. You just do it. Like you moving to Chicago. Hell, you didn't know a soul there. You just wanted to be there, so you went, and you made it happen. I bet that quality proved helpful as a reporter. I bet you were willing to do whatever it took to get your story. You probably jumped right in and took risks that other journalists might not have been willing to take."

It was true. I'd been promoted through the ranks at the station at a younger age than anyone ever had been, mostly due to my willingness to take risks and my tenacity to make things happen.

"How do you do that?" I asked Seth. "How do you always seem to see the best in me? Even after everything I put you through?"

"Headlights," he said, staring in the rearview mirror. "Best to get down, just in case."

I crouched low in the seat again, but my eyes never left Seth's face. How had I been dumb enough to walk away from him? How had I ever thought my life was better without him?

"They don't seem to be getting any closer, but I'm not taking any chances. Hold on. I'm making a right turn."

He turned, and then he watched the rearview mirror, his jaw tight and his face tense.

"Okay, they went past and didn't turn."

The lights of a gas station became visible in the distance, and Seth slowed the car as we approached it.

"At the risk of sounding like the dumb female sidekick who gets everyone killed in the movie, I have to pee," I said. "I hadn't wanted to mention it before, but since we're stopping anyway..."

"It's all that damn whiskey you drank," he said with a grin. "Let me pump the gas, and then I'll take you to the restroom."

"Um, there's no one here other than the cashier. I think I could go by myself."

"No," he said with a shake of his head. "I don't want us separated, just in case someone shows up."

"Right."

As it turned out, the restroom was on the back of the building, and the light back there buzzed loudly but gave off little illumination. It was spooky as hell, and even if we hadn't been hunted at the moment, I would have been relieved to have Seth walk back there with me.

"I'll be right out here," he said once he'd opened the door to the restroom and turned on the light to ensure no one was inside. "I'm gonna walk back to the corner so I can see if anyone pulls up or goes near the car, but I'll be able to see this door at all times."

"Thanks, Seth. I appreciate all you're doing to keep me safe. I'm so sorry I dragged you into all this." On impulse, I stepped toward him and wrapped my arms around his neck. "I might have been a fool to marry Victor, but I was a bigger fool to let you go."

I moved to kiss him, and he stepped back, gently freeing himself from my embrace.

"I can't afford to get distracted and get us both killed. Hurry up, okay? I want to keep moving."

SEVEN

He was on the phone when I came out of the restroom, and he ended the call in hushed tones as I walked toward him.

"Everything okay?" I asked.

"Yeah. Tristan's been by your folks' place and Amy's a couple of times so far, but no sign of anyone. He'll keep checking. Don't worry."

"So, where are we headed?"

"In a few more circles for right now," he said as we made our way back to the car. "I want to make sure we're not being followed before I land somewhere for the night."

His face looked haggard under the bright fluorescent lights of the canopy over the pumps.

"You worked today, right?" I asked, and he nodded. "Were you up early?"

"Four."

"Damn. Yeah. That's early. You must be tired."

"I'm okay. Adrenaline works wonders to keep you awake when you need to be."

He wasn't kidding when he said he intended to drive in circles. He made so many twists, turns, detours, and U-turns that I didn't even know where we were, and we were driving roads I'd known my whole life.

"So, what about you?" I said after a while. "You never married, huh?"

"Nope. Always been a bachelor."

"Did you ever come close?" Though it was unfair and not my right, I felt a pang of jealousy toward any unknown woman who had held his heart in that way.

He flashed a weak smile in my direction and shook his head. "No."

"Really?" I found it hard to believe such a great guy hadn't been close to the altar. He was handsome, hardworking, honest, loyal, funny, affectionate, and *not* a member of the Mafia. Always a plus. "C'mon, no one tempted you to take the plunge? What about that girl —what was her name? It was a car name. Oh, Nova! What about Nova?"

His eyes were wide as he looked at me. "How do you know about Nova?"

"Amy told me." I smiled and looked away. "I might have asked about you from time to time. Curiosity, I suppose."

He chuckled, and I turned back to him with a grin.

"What? Are you gonna tell me you never asked about me? You knew I got married and that I was divorced, and you said you knew Victor had never been back here to visit with me. So, you must have been keeping some kind of tabs."

"Like anyone can escape the news in Cedar Creek. I had, like, fifty people tell me the minute you were back in town."

"I guess we'll always be linked in everyone's mind, huh?" My heart beat faster at the thought.

"Yeah, I guess so."

"Spill the beans. What about this Nova chick? Why didn't you want to marry her?" Part of me didn't want to hear about his relationship with another woman, but a bigger part of me wondered why he'd stayed single all this time.

"Nova's a nice enough girl. She'll make someone a great wife someday, but she wasn't the one for me. I'm thinking you might need to turn your phone back on. Victor said he'll call in an hour, and it's been longer than that."

"I told you I don't want to talk to him."

"I know, but he may have left a message. We need to know where Victor is and if he plans to come here to meet you."

"I'm not meeting him. What do I have to say to convince you that's not what this is about?"

"I believe you, but he said he'd explain when he saw you. You might not intend to see him, but evidently, he intends to see you. If you're right that he escaped federal prison to come to you, he's not going to give up easily. The good thing is he'll be hunted, if he's not being hunted already. We need to lay low until he's caught. In the meantime, I'd feel better knowing where he is and where he thinks you'll be, so I can get you as far away from that as possible."

"But don't you see? Even if they catch Victor, even if they send him back, I'm still in the crosshairs. He said these people are angry with him, and they intend to hurt me to get revenge. If we elude whoever it was tonight, they'll just send someone else. I'm never going to be safe." My voice cracked with the realization. "It won't ever be okay for me to go back home, will it? Not without putting the people I love in danger."

Seth took my hand and squeezed it. "I won't let anything happen to you, and Tristan won't let anything happen to your family."

"But you and Tristan can't always be there, Seth. What are we going to do? Run away and hide forever?"

"We don't have to hide forever, just until this blows over. Just until Victor is caught."

"But Victor isn't the one trying to kill me! Did you forget that?"

He grimaced, and I sensed there was something he wanted to say but was holding back.

"What? Tell me. If you know something, you have to tell me, Seth. What is it?"

"I'm not so sure there's someone after you."

"What do you mean? Victor said my life was in danger. He said—"

"And yet, we haven't seen anyone. No one. No one was waiting outside your house. No one followed us out of town. We've been driving for hours with no sign of a threat."

"Yeah, but you yourself said you've been going in circles so no one could find us. You got us away from whoever it was."

"Then why hasn't Tristan seen anyone unusual near your family or near your house?"

I pulled my hand from his. "What are you saying?"

He shrugged. "The only person who stands to gain from you leaving in a panic and not telling anyone is Victor."

"You think he lied to get me to leave my house? Why? Why would he do that?"

"Well, from what you've told me, he has no qualms with lying to you, or with hiding things from you, at the least. If he planned to make a break from prison, he's likely planning to leave the country or to go underground and change his identity. Either way, I think he wants you to accompany him."

"What? That's ridiculous. There's no way I would do that."

He shrugged again. "Unless you were scared. Unless you feared for your life and your family's life. Unless you thought he was the only one who could protect you."

Victor might have kept the truth from me about his nefarious alternate life, but he'd never done anything to harm me. I couldn't conceive of him doing something so manipulative, so vile.

"He wouldn't do that. He wouldn't scare the crap out of me to make me take him back. He wouldn't make me think my family was in danger, that I was in danger. You didn't hear his voice, Seth. He was frantic. He sounded terrified for me. There was such a sense of urgency in his tone."

"Which makes sense when you consider that he'd just escaped prison and needed to set things in motion as quickly as possible."

"No." I shook my head, unwilling to believe what seemed to be true. It had been hard enough believing my ex-husband was a killer. Believing he'd kept an entirely different life hidden from me. It had been painful to consider that our love wasn't what I thought it had been, that our life was likely a cover. A sham. But I couldn't believe he would willingly lie in order to take me from my family and make me come to him out of fear. I couldn't accept that he would knowingly hurt me after all he'd put me through.

"Think about what this guy is capable of," Seth said. "The level of dishonesty he's capable of."

"You don't know him. You didn't hear the way he apologized as they led him away. The way he kept screaming that he loved me over and over again. He wouldn't do something like this to me. He wouldn't. He hid that life to protect me from it. He called and warned me because he thought my life was in danger. He loves me," I declared, even though I'd questioned whether it was true since the moment I found out about Victor's other life.

"I have no doubt that he does," Seth said. "If the man has the contacts and the resources to pull off a bust out of federal custody, and he chooses to make a detour for you, then obviously, he feels like life on the outside isn't worth living without you. But that makes him all the more dangerous, because he's got limited options. He doesn't have time to convince you to come with him. He has to make you come by whatever means necessary, and then convince you to forgive him later."

I pressed my palms against my eyes, trying to shut out the truth and keep the tears at bay. I refused to shed another tear due to Victor Gallo, but my wounded heart felt as though it might cave in on itself. Another betrayal. Another layer of lies. Another manipulation of my feelings and my trust.

Then another thought popped into my head, something I'd almost forgotten in the madness of the night. I still didn't know for sure who Metro Man was or his purpose in Cedar Creek.

"Wait, wait, wait. Victor said someone had been watching me, and I think that's true. I've gotten that sensation several times, and strange things have happened. Nothing major, and nothing concrete, you know? Stuff like, I'd come home one day to find the creamer out on the kitchen counter, even though I was certain I'd put it away that morning. Another time, I left the house before the newspaper got delivered, but when I came home, it was out of its plastic sleeve and folded on the dining table. Both times, along with a few others I can't think of specifically right now, I'd been distracted. Busy. Not sleeping well. So, I convinced myself I'd simply forgotten doing it or had been mistaken in my memory of things. But then there was Metro Man."

"Who?

"Metro Man. That's not his name, of course. I don't know his name. He's this guy I saw in the grocery store a week or so ago, and then again tonight in the bar. He stood out to me because of the way he was dressed. Definitely not from around here."

"Oh, are you talking about the dude in the corner with the man bun and the high-water pants?"

"Yeah!" I turned in the seat, excited at his immediate recognition. "Do you know him?"

"No. I saw him at the bar, and like you said, he stood out, but I've never seen him before tonight. When you saw him at the grocery store, did he approach you? Say anything to you? Follow you out to your car?"

"No, nothing like that. It was more of a feeling than anything else. That eerie sense that someone is watching you. That they're only there because you are. I brushed it off when I didn't see him again, but then tonight, he was in the bar, sitting alone and not drinking what he'd ordered."

"Did he make any contact with you tonight?"

"Not really. He bought me a drink, but he left before I even got it."

"What do you mean?" Seth's brows furrowed. "So, you met him? You talked to him?"

I shook my head. "No. We made eye contact a couple of times, and he lifted his drink in, like, I don't know, *acknowledgment* that we kept looking at each other, I guess? Then, Shannon came over and told me the guy wanted to buy me a round. I figured then he'd gotten the wrong idea and thought I was interested, but when I turned back, he'd gone. He left and didn't come back in."

Seth twisted his hands back and forth on the steering wheel and drew in a deep breath as he considered my words.

"What?" I asked when his silence lingered. "What are you thinking?"

"Is that why you came over to talk to me? You felt threatened by this guy or wanted to throw him off?"

"What? No! Of course not! He'd already gone when I came over to talk to you, and if I'd still thought at that point he was a hitman, I wouldn't have involved you. In fact, that's part of the reason I told you not to sit by me. I didn't want you to get caught up in this mess if he was what I thought." Frowning, I rested my elbow against the door and propped my head in my hand. "A lot of good that did. I ended up getting you involved anyway."

"I don't think this changes anything. If, um—what did you call the guy?"

"Metro Man."

"Okay, if *Metro Man* had been following you or out to get you, why would he buy you a drink and bring attention to himself? Why wouldn't he be waiting at your house? Why wouldn't he follow us when we left? The guy's probably an investor looking for real estate in the suburbs like every other yahoo with money to burn, and he thought he was about to get lucky and score. So, he bought you a drink, saw your reaction when Shannon told you, and left without being rejected."

"You may be right, but even if Metro Man wasn't a bad guy, I still believe Victor was telling the truth when he said they'd been in my house. If anything, he only confirmed what I already suspected and didn't want to face and acknowledge. I've got a Mafia target on my back."

"Maybe, maybe not. It's possible you were being watched, but the people watching you were doing so *for* Victor, not because of him."

I turned toward the window and covered my face with my hand, trying to fight back tears but too overwhelmed to keep them all from escaping.

"Hey," Seth said, reaching to rub the back of my neck. "I'm sorry. I don't know whether it makes it easier or harder for you to think this Victor guy is pulling all the strings. I wish I knew for sure, and I wish I could make it all go away for you. But I can't ignore what my instinct is telling me on this one, and I can't protect you if I'm not being realistic about who I think is the greatest threat we're facing."

"I'm okay," I said, moving my hands away from my eyes as I blinked rapidly and nodded to convince myself. "I'm fine. Hey, this makes things easier, right? We just have to wait it out until the authorities catch Victor, and then once he's back in prison, I'm safe, right? So, where do we go to hide?"

He kept his hand on the back of my neck, his thumb lightly stroking my hair line as he stared at the road ahead of us.

"I think we should let Tristan in on everything. I think we let him use the system and the resources he has to put things in motion, to find out for sure if Victor has escaped, and if so, to put out a high alert. If Victor's planning to get to you as soon as possible, he's likely flying, and he'd use a smaller airport."

"His uncle has a private jet. He had planned to fly me to New York City for Christmas, but he was arrested before the holidays came."

Moving his hand back to the steering wheel, he nodded. "Okay. He told you to drive north, and that he'd give you more instructions in an hour. Based on the distance from Cedar Creek, I'm thinking that means he intends to land in Ocala. If we can figure out where, maybe we could have people ready to greet Victor and put him back in handcuffs when he lands."

My thoughts and emotions jumbled together in a mental train wreck as I tried to sort through it all and determine what was valid.

Had Victor lied to me? Had he threatened my life and the lives of my family to make me do what he wanted? Knowing I would never come to him willingly, had he used the people I loved to manipulate me? And if I still refused to accompany him, what then? Would he take me against my will?

My anger at being used and my frustration with my gullibility in believing him was only tempered by the very real possibility that he was telling the truth.

"Okay," I said to Seth, pressing my fingers against my temples to try and stop my mind from spinning. "So, best-case scenario, my ex-husband busted out of jail and is on his way to pick me up, and he lied to make me run away with him. In that scenario, my family isn't in danger, but I could possibly be kidnapped and taken out of the country against my will."

"I won't let that happen."

I ignored him and continued with my situation inventory.

"Worst-case scenario, my ex-husband busted out of jail and is on his way to pick me up, but he was telling the truth, and hit men from one of the world's most powerful organized crime families are after me and might kill my family if they can't find me." I turned to look at Seth as my entire body began to tremble again. "Are there any options I'm not seeing here? Anything where I'm not likely to die or get someone I love killed?"

He reached to cup my cheek in his hand. "I won't let him take you. I won't let anyone take you. And if they intend to hurt you, they have to come through me."

I tilted my head to press my face into his hand as I tried to smile. "I appreciate that, and I have no doubt you would put up the most valiant effort that's ever been waged. But Seth, the truth of the matter is, it's just the two of us against the Mafia in both of those scenarios, and the odds don't seem to be in our favor."

"Not if you let me make that call. Let me get my team on this. Let them work to find Victor and nullify that threat."

"And what if you're wrong? What if Victor was telling the truth and he really was trying to save my life, and in return, we lock him up and send him back to prison, but I'm not any safer?"

"Yet another reason we need to get more people involved. We're driving blind here. We don't know what we're up against."

I took in a deep breath and held it as I closed my eyes, wishing I could click my heels together and be someplace else. Someone else. But when I opened my eyes, I was still Dani Ward. And I still had to live out the consequences of my choices.

"What do you need me to do?" I asked, ready to move forward since there didn't seem to be any other option.

"Turn on your phone, and let's see if there's any message from Victor."

He had called exactly one hour after the initial call, just as he said he would.

His message was cryptic, as one might expect from an escaped convict not wanting to be caught.

"Your phone went straight to voicemail, so I hope you're okay. I understand if you're mad at me, sweetness. Really, I do. You have every right to be. But what matters most now is your safety. Hopefully, you've been driving north for the past hour. Call me when you get this and let me know your location. I can have someone come to you and make sure you're protected. Start the sand."

"What does he mean about the sand?" Seth asked as the message ended.

We'd been listening via Bluetooth through the car's stereo system, and I turned the phone back off and shoved it in my purse.

"The sand means he'll see me soon. I had a small hourglass on the bookshelves in my house in Chicago. It was, um, a thing between us. When I would leave the station to head home at night, I'd tell him to start the sand as a visual reminder that I'd see him soon. A countdown, of sorts."

"How long would that be? The countdown? How long did it take you to get home from work?"

"Right at an hour."

He leaned forward to cross his arms across the top of the steering wheel.

"All right, so if I'm right about him flying to Ocala from the Chicago area, that should be a little more than two hours flight time, which fits the timetable if he called you the first time before he took off and the second time mid-air."

"If that's the case, he'd be landing in roughly forty-five minutes, right?"

"Give or take." Seth sat up straighter, tapping his index fingers against the steering wheel as he mulled over everything. "You told him you don't want to talk to him and you don't want to see him, but he's obviously holding out hope that you'll change your mind. He has to assume you might turn him in, so it's not likely he'd leave a message of where he's going to be. He'd rather you give him a location and then he can send his people to you and have them check out the situation. They'll either give you further instruction or bring you to him."

"You say this like I'm actually going. I'm not, right? You won't make me go meet him just to catch him, will you?"

His sideways glance made me fear he had considered it, but then he grabbed my hand and pulled it to his lips, squeezing it tight against his mouth as he shook his head. "No. I would never put you in that situation. I'd never risk your life like that."

Any relief I might have felt was overtaken by anxiety about what would happen instead.

"Then what do we do? What's the grand plan?"

"I can't imagine this guy would fly right into Ocala's regional airport. That's way too easy to trace and to intercept. More than likely, he'll land on someone's private airstrip. The Ocala area has plenty of those."

"How will we know where he's going to land?"

"Let me call Tristan and update him with what we have. I'd like to find Victor in the air and track him on the way down. Have the handcuffs waiting for him."

"What if he knows I made that happen?" I asked, the fear rising in my throat like hot bile. "What if he retaliates against me?"

"If he's no longer in federal custody, then some kind of alarm has to have been raised. If we can apprehend him when he lands, then there's no way for him to tie that to you."

"But if I don't call him back…"

"Hey, don't go down that path, okay? Stay focused. Right now, we need to find out where Victor is."

He picked up his phone to dial Tristan, and I leaned forward to put my head between my knees as the world began to spin and turn black around the edges.

EIGHT

Though I could only hear one side of the conversation, Tristan obviously already knew the most pertinent facts of our situation. Seth must have told him when they talked while I was in the service station restroom earlier.

While I understood why he did it, I still felt betrayed that he had.

"Why ask my permission to involve him if you knew you'd already done so?" I asked Seth once he'd ended their call.

"I involved him when I asked him to check on your family. You gave me permission to do that."

"Yes, but I also told you I can't trust anyone in law enforcement right now, and I can't risk the Mafia thinking I went to the cops."

He looked over at me with a sigh. "You trust me, don't you?"

"Of course."

"Okay, then you know that I wouldn't do anything to put you in danger. Once you told me who we were running from, I needed an extra set of eyes and ears. I can't just keep driving in circles and hope they never find us. If I'm gonna keep you safe, I need someone actively looking for Victor while we're hiding from him."

"And you trust Tristan?"

"I do," he said, glancing over at me and then back at the road. "With my life. And yours."

Tristan hadn't grown up in Cedar Creek, so I only knew him through my friend and business partner Sloane, who was engaged to him. She trusted him, and I trusted her. Seth trusted him, and I trusted Seth. So, I suppose the next logical step was for me to trust Tristan. It wasn't like I had a choice at this point.

"He knows to be discreet, right? He knows not to tell anyone else, right? You warned him that—"

"Tristan knows, okay?"

I gave a quick nod and set aside that concern for a much larger one.

"Did he find out anything about Victor?"

Seth frowned. "There's been no report of him escaping."

"But he said he'd see me. I don't understand. You're saying he's still in prison? Then, I'm safe, right?"

"Not exactly," Seth said, his frown deepening. "Just because it hasn't been reported doesn't mean it hasn't happened. If Victor's associates wanted him out badly enough, they could have paid for silence to buy him time to reach his destination."

If no one knew Victor had escaped, then no one was searching for him. And that meant not only was I still in danger, but there was no cavalry on its way to catch the bad guy. My fears accelerated, and I picked my feet up into the seat and wrapped my arms around my knees in an effort to comfort myself.

"What do we do now?"

Seth reached to rub his hand across my knee with a light squeeze.

"We're gonna find a place to stop and get some rest."

"What?" My voice shot up an octave in my panic, and my feet slammed back down to the floor. "You're stopping? Are you crazy? I thought we needed to keep moving."

"That was when we thought someone was chasing us. We've driven in every circle and detour I can take us on with no sign of anyone on our tail. Victor told you to head north, right? We're an hour south of Cedar Creek instead, roughly two hours from where he thinks you'll be. That buys us a little time to find him and being in one place makes it easier for me to get backup if we need it."

It made sense, and I knew Seth wouldn't take unnecessary chances, but the prospect of sitting and waiting felt more scary than being on the move somehow.

That prospect got even worse when Seth pulled into the parking lot of a one-story budget motel long past its prime.

"Whoa. Seriously?" I leaned forward to get a closer look and wished I hadn't. "They're bound to have nicer places if you keep driving a little farther."

He grinned at my obvious disgust.

"Hey, it's not like we're checking in for a vacation, okay? I want to be able to park the car right in front of the room so I can see the parking lot and get in and out quickly if we need to. If you'll notice, there are several bars surrounding this place, including one attached to the lobby. That gives us people moving around for the next couple of hours, and that's a good thing. We want witnesses. We don't want to be any place that's deserted or where everyone around us is sleeping soundly."

I frowned at the strains of music coming from the bar as Seth cut off the engine. "Yeah, I don't think anyone is sleeping soundly here, that's for sure. But I thought we were stopping because you don't think anyone's following us and you don't expect Victor to know where we are. Why can't we stay some place nicer?"

"What if I'm wrong? Would he look for you someplace like this?" He arched an eyebrow, and his grin widened. I didn't even have to answer. He already knew.

Seth used his name and credit card for the room to keep me from being attached to it, and as I waited for him to get the key, I wandered over towards the cased opening that led into the bar. A smoky haze hovered inside the dark room, which was crowded and boisterous. I found it hard to believe that a couple of hours ago, I'd been like these people—kicking back with a drink to let off steam on a Friday night.

Now, I was running for my life from the Mafia, hiding from my escaped gangster ex-husband, and checking into a questionable hotel with the same guy I'd given my virginity to way back in high school.

If all that wasn't deserving of a drink, I didn't know what was.

"Ready?" Seth asked as he came to my side. "I was able to get a first-floor room relatively close to the lobby, hopefully far enough away that we don't hear this music but close enough that we could be seen by witnesses if we need to be."

I looped my arm through his and smiled. "You wanna get a drink? My treat. It's the least I can do."

He scanned the bar and frowned. "I don't know if that's such a good idea. We should probably head back to the room and settle in. I need to let Tristan know where we are and see if he has any update on Victor."

"C'mon. One drink. What is one drink gonna hurt? No one followed us here, and Victor has no idea where we are. This seems to be the only entrance, so you'll be able to see anyone who comes in. Besides, you said witnesses are good. This place is full of witnesses. Wouldn't we be safer here than in the room all by ourselves?"

His frown didn't disappear, but he took another look at the room, which told me he was considering my suggestion.

"Please?" I asked, squeezing his arm. "The last couple of hours have been so stressful, and I just want to forget all that for a little bit. Have one drink with me, and then we'll go to our crappy little room and hide until the good guys catch the bad guys and it's safe to go home again."

Even as I said it, I knew there were no guarantees it would happen. If Victor couldn't be found, and we couldn't verify whether my life was in danger from another source, then it wouldn't be safe to go home. Not tonight, and maybe not ever.

My face must have revealed the turmoil of my inner thoughts, because Seth reached to stroke his knuckles across my cheek, and then he tucked his thumb under my chin. "Would your smile come back if we had one drink?"

I nodded, forcing my face into a grin to reassure him as he took my hand and led me inside the bar.

We found a hi-top cocktail table with an unobstructed view of the entrance, and we had just settled onto the stools when a waitress stopped and took our drink orders.

As if the night didn't already feel surreal enough with me sitting on a barstool next to Seth, the next song the DJ in the corner played was an old Dixie Chicks hit that had been *our song* back in the day.

He looked at me and grinned, and I laughed.

"What are the chances?" he asked, shaking his head in disbelief.

"Well? What do you say, cowboy? You gonna take me away to the dance floor for old times' sake?"

His eyes held mine, and it was as though I could see straight through them and into his mind as he debated all the reasons he shouldn't.

Certain he was about to refuse, I'd already prepared myself for the rejection, but then he stood and took my hand to pull me onto the dance floor.

I wrapped my arms around his neck as his arms encircled my waist, and we swayed back and forth to the music of our past, the lyrics tangled with the memories of young love and the promises we'd made and been unable to keep.

Seth's eyes never left mine as our bodies slowly inched closer together, and when there was no space left between us, he bent his forehead to mine with a soft swear beneath his breath.

"What?" I asked, even though I worried I might not want to know.

He squeezed his arms tighter around me, pulling me in even closer somehow. "It feels so good to hold you again, and yet, at the same time..."

I waited for his words to come, waited for him to say any one of the reasons that it wasn't a good idea for me to be in his arms, and I knew no matter which one he picked, I wouldn't be able to argue. I was no good for Seth. I hadn't been then, and I surely wasn't now.

But he didn't finish his thought. He just sighed, running his hand up my back as he pressed his lips to my temple and then rested his cheek against my hair. He held me so tightly that it was hard to breathe, but I didn't care about oxygen. I clung to him, savoring every second and fearing that when the song ended, we would part and never find our way back to a moment like this again.

"It damned near killed me when you left," he whispered near my ear as the last notes of the song played out. "I wanted to go after you so badly, but I knew my family needed me here, and I guess I thought you'd come back. That maybe you needed me too, but you never did."

I pulled back to look up at him, desperate to see his eyes, but then recoiling from the raw pain I found there.

"Seth, I did need you. More than you know. I was just too damned stubborn to admit it. I never should have made you choose like that. It was selfish and unfair, and I'm sorry."

The song had ended, and though another had begun, we stood motionless in the middle of the dance floor, still holding each other.

"I thought I was over you," he said, his voice hoarse with emotion. "When I heard you'd moved back to town, I thought it would be fine. I figured we'd see each other around, and we could be cordial—friendly even—and I'd be okay. But then you seemed so angry at me when I saw you, and—"

"It wasn't you, Seth; it was me. I was angry with myself for all the mistakes I've made, and I was scared of what I would feel being around you. I know that sounds ridiculous after I was the one who left and all the time that's passed—"

"Hell, it's like no time has passed at all. Having you in my arms again, I know why no one else has ever worked out. I meant it when I said you took my heart when you left, and I've never gotten it back. It's always been yours. I'm scared it always will be."

Another couple bumped into us as they spun in time to the music, and it brought Seth's attention back to our present situation. His body stiffened as his eyes scanned the room, and though I clung tighter, he pulled away.

"We should get to the room and get out of sight," he said, his voice gruff. The tenderness and vulnerability were gone.

The waitress had just arrived with our drinks as we reached the table, and I reached into my purse to pay, but Seth shook his head and pulled money from his pocket to give her. I turned the glass of whiskey up and drained it, wincing at the burn in my throat as Seth grabbed my hand again and began to walk towards the door.

"Wait, Seth, what about your beer? You didn't even touch it."

"I don't need to be any more distracted than I already am."

He pulled me through the crowd without once looking back, and I yanked on his arm to stop him when we reached the lobby.

"What's wrong?"

"We need to keep moving."

I fell in step beside him but wasn't willing to let it go.

"Fine, but can you please tell me why you're angry?"

He reached his arm across my torso and gently pushed me behind him as he stepped up to the double glass doors, peering out toward the parking lot.

Evidently satisfied there was no danger, he stepped outside, and we walked at a rapid pace down the sidewalk with Seth turning left and right constantly to watch in all directions.

His heightened sense of awareness alarmed me and reminded me of the reason we were there. While we were dancing, it had been so easy to forget that people were after me. For the length of the song, it had been like my life was back to normal, and I'd never screwed up and married the mob.

When we arrived at our room, I was surprised to see Seth pull out an actual key.

"Wow. Do all motels still use real keys instead of key cards you swipe?"

He shrugged as he slid the key into the lock. "I don't know. I can't tell you the last time I checked into a motel."

After unlocking the door and checking the room with his pistol drawn, Seth motioned for me to come inside, and then he shut the door and slid the deadbolt in place.

The hotel's interior had been redone more recently than its exterior, and it wasn't as bad as I'd feared. There were two queen beds with gold and green striped comforters that seemed fairly new. The nightstand between them held a telephone and a lamp with charging ports on either side of its base. A single dresser sat across from the beds. It had a flatscreen television on top of it, and a mini refrigerator on the floor beside it.

I sat on one of the beds as Seth pulled the gold and green striped drapes shut and moved the gold armchair from the corner and placed it in front of the door, lodging it beneath the knob.

"Are you ever going to tell me why you got so mad back there?"

He turned and stared at me with his hands on his hips, his lips in a grim line and his brow furrowed.

"I'm not mad, D. Well, not at you, at least. Myself, for sure. I let my guard down, and I can't afford to do that."

For a moment, I wasn't sure if he meant he'd let it down with his feelings for me or with our current dire situation, but his next sentence clarified things.

"I could get us both killed if I don't keep my head in the game."

The fear that had returned when we were outside began to ramp up, and my heart started racing again.

"I thought you said we should be safe. Victor doesn't know where we are, and since no one was following us, they don't have a way to find us, right?"

"Until we know where he is and that he can't get to you, we need to stay alert." He came and sat on the bed beside me, reaching to tuck my hair behind my ear and brush it back off my shoulder. "I'm sorry, okay?" He took my hand and intertwined our fingers. "I won't let myself get distracted again."

I hesitated before nodding. While I certainly didn't want either of us harmed, I also wouldn't mind him being distracted if it meant he would hold me.

He squeezed my hand before releasing it. "Why don't you try to get some sleep?"

With a scoffing laugh, I looked back at him. "There's no way I can sleep right now."

"I understand," he said, standing. "I need to call Tristan and see if he has any update, and I want to let him know where we are, just in case we need him."

"Is he still keeping an eye on my family?"

Seth nodded. "Yeah. He's got someone watching their houses."

I opened my mouth to protest, but he lifted his hand and answered the question before I asked it.

"He didn't tell anyone anything. He just put your parents and Amy under patrol watch."

"And no one asked why?"

"After you work with people a while in the situations we get into, you learn who you can trust without having to ask a bunch of questions."

Despite my declaration that I wouldn't be able to sleep, a yawn escaped me, and I stood and stretched.

"I think I'm gonna take a hot shower. Maybe that will help me relax. I just wish I'd had time to pack a change of clothes so I didn't have to put these back on when I get out."

"Maybe there's a robe in the bathroom."

Laughing at the lunacy of his suggestion, I walked to the bathroom and looked behind the door to be sure I was right before stating the obvious. "This is not the type of hotel that offers lush robes. Hell, it's not even a hotel at all. It's a motel."

"When did you get all hoity-toity?" he asked with a grin. "I remember staying in quite a few motels with you back in the day. Road trips. Beach trips. Concerts."

"Yeah, because we were broke college students, and we'd rather spend our money on beer back then, so we'd get the cheapest place possible and pile as many people into the room as we could to divide up the cost. I like to think my life progressed past needing to stay in cheap motels." Even as I said it, the reality of my finances brought me up short. Since I'd lost my job and had all my accounts frozen by the feds, I'd been teetering on the brink of bankruptcy, and if my attorney didn't get things freed up soon, I'd have much bigger worries than hotels and motels.

Of course, if my ex-husband or someone in his organization killed me, then money would no longer be a concern.

Neither outcome seemed appealing, and I frowned as I gathered a towel and washcloth from the rack above the sink. Once I'd pulled back the thin shower curtain and twisted the knob to turn on the water, I realized I didn't have any toiletries.

"Great," I said as I turned the water off and came back out to where Seth still sat on the bed, typing a text on his phone. "Not only do I not have any clean clothes, but I have no way to get clean. Not a shampoo bottle or bar of soap in sight."

"They probably have them at the front desk. I'll call and see if we can have some delivered. What do you need?"

"Whatever they have. Shampoo. Soap. Conditioner. I'd love a toothbrush and some toothpaste if I could get it. Maybe a razor and some shaving cream?"

He laughed as he picked up the handset of the motel's phone. "You don't ask for much. You want me to see if they have a stylist who could come and fix your hair while we're at it? Maybe they could send a masseuse as well?"

"What's wrong with my hair?" Defensively, I lifted my hand to touch it and turned to get a glimpse in the mirror as Seth talked to the front desk clerk.

To say I looked like hell was an understatement. The tears I'd cried earlier had erased most of my make-up, leaving my face pale and splotchy. Remnants of mascara and liner had left black smudges beneath my eyes, and my long, brown hair was in desperate need of a brushing. I wet my finger and rubbed at a particularly large smudge at the corner of my left eye, but that only served to smear it worse.

"Okay," Seth said as he hung up the phone. "Here's the deal.

They have shampoo, soap, and some kind of finger brush with a toothpaste tablet."

"That sounds gross."

"Yeah, well, better than nothing, I suppose. The front office clerk is the only person on staff at this hour, so he can't bring the stuff. I have to go get it. I want you to deadbolt the door and put the chair back under the knob as soon as I'm out, okay? Don't open it for any reason. Here," he said, grabbing the pencil and pad from the night-stand and scribbling out a number. "This is Tristan's cell number. If I'm not back—"

"No, forget it. I don't want you to leave the room."

"I'll be fine. But I want you to take the precautions and have his number, just in case."

"I don't need a shower. I know I've been griping and complain-ing, but it's okay, really. I'd rather have you safe."

He walked to the window and pulled back the curtain enough to look outside.

"I don't see any vehicles that weren't here when we got here. A few have left, but that's to be expected because the bar should be closing soon. I'll be back in five minutes."

"No, I don't want you to go. If something happened to you because I wanted shampoo and a toothpaste tablet, I'd never forgive myself."

"Nothing's going to happen to me. Besides, I'd like a toothpaste tablet of my own, okay? And maybe I'll see if I can find a bottle of water in a vending machine."

"Oh, I'd love some water. Can you bring back ice?" I grabbed the ice bucket from the top of the dresser and handed it to him.

"I love how you went from it not being safe for me to go to '*please bring back ice*' in the span of, like, two seconds."

He smiled, and I smiled back.

"I'd still rather you not go," I said, "but if there's anyone more stubborn than me, it's you. So I know you're gonna go, and you might as well bring me some ice for my whiskey."

Shaking his head with a chuckle, he shoved his pistol in the back of his waistband and walked toward the door.

"Wait until I'm back to get in the shower, okay? I want you aware of your surroundings. And keep this door locked with the chair in front of it. Don't open it for anyone."

"Yes, sir," I said with a dramatic salute. "Got it."

Our eyes locked as he stood with his hand on the knob, and then on impulse, I rushed forward and wrapped my arms around his neck, pressing my lips to his.

"It's gonna be fine," he whispered as he hugged me to him and then released me. "Don't worry. I'll be back in five."

NINE

I paced back and forth between the door and the window once he'd gone, stopping to peer out through the curtains each time I passed the window and putting my knee on the chair to look out the peephole each time I reached the door.

Even though I knew he hadn't meant five minutes literally, I couldn't help checking the time every few seconds. Frustrated with how long it took the digital number on my watch to change from minute to minute, I used the stopwatch feature instead so I could see the progress.

It had barely gone over six minutes and I was almost back to the door when I heard someone outside. Pressing my eye to the peephole, I could see Seth juggling the ice bucket and two bottles of water as he pulled the key from his pocket.

I tossed my cell phone onto the chair and scooted it back out of the way so I could twist the deadbolt to jerk the door open. He'd stuck the key in the lock far enough for the sudden movement of the door to pull the key from his hand, but not far enough for the lock to hold it, and the key fell to the ground between us.

We both went to retrieve it at the same time, and as he bent, the shampoo and toothbrush fell from the top of the ice bucket along with a Baby Ruth candy bar, which had been my favorite back in the day.

I grinned as I grabbed it from the ground. "You brought me a Baby Ruth?"

As my head came up to look at him, a blur of movement from the left surged forward, and then everything happened all at once.

Ice scattered across the ground as the man who'd pounced on a still crouching Seth pounded him into the concrete, and then out of nowhere there were two more men, kicking and punching Seth as he put up a valiant resistance from the ground.

My own scream sounded like it came from far away, not even connected with my body. Seth yelled at me to run, but it was too late. One of the men had already turned to come for me. I scrambled to move backward into the room and shut the door, but I'd forgotten about the chair, and I stumbled and fell back across it before rolling off onto the floor.

I flipped onto my stomach and began to crawl toward the phone on the nightstand, screaming at the top of my lungs until a gloved hand clamped down over my mouth and a knee in my back knocked the breath from me and pinned me to the carpet between the two beds.

"Let her go. Get your hands off her," said a voice I knew well and would recognize anywhere. I wasn't sure whether to feel relieved or more terrified as the hand moved away from my mouth and the knee released me to roll over and stare up at my ex-husband.

"She was screaming," said the man who'd held me.

"Move," Victor ordered, and the man stepped aside for Victor to reach down and help me up. He wrapped me in his arms so tightly I couldn't breathe. "Oh, God, sweetness. It feels so good to hold you."

I pushed him away and stood staring at the man I'd vowed to spend the rest of my life with, the man I thought I'd known and been sure I'd loved.

During the two years since Victor had been dragged away from our house in handcuffs, I'd often thought about what it would be like to see him again. I'd wondered if I would still find him attractive, if our explosive chemistry would still be impossible to deny. My reaction to him when we'd first met had been unlike anything I'd ever experienced, and I'd feared that somehow the flame would still be there in spite of all I'd learned about him. It was part of the reason I'd refused to visit him in prison, had allowed his calls to go unanswered, and had tossed his letters in the trash unopened. I didn't want to discover that I could be attracted to a killer who had betrayed me.

In a matter of seconds, all those concerns vanished. Though he looked much the same as he had the morning they'd led him away, I saw him through a different lens. Whereas before, one look at him could send quivers of desire rippling through me and make me shiver in anticipation of his touch, now I felt nothing but contempt and disgust, layered over an undercurrent of fear.

He smiled his crooked smile, and a wave of nausea rolled through me.

"He's a cop, boss," said one of Victor's men behind me, and I turned to see him holding up Seth's wallet and pistol as the other two dragged a motionless and bloodied Seth across the threshold into the room. "Carrying a badge."

I tried to go to Seth, but Victor grabbed me by the shoulders and bent to stare into my eyes. "Are you okay? Did this cop harass you? Did he hurt you?"

Incredulous at his suggestion and still in shock from the turn of events, I stared at him wide-eyed. "What? No! Of course not."

"God, it kills me to see the fear in your eyes," he said, pulling me back against him. "It's okay. I'm here now. You're safe. I won't let anything happen to you."

My brain seemed stuck in slow motion, unable to process everything happening until the man standing over Seth asked, "What do you want us to do with him? Should we get rid of him?"

"No!" I shoved Victor with all my might and ran past him to kneel at Seth's side. Blood seeped from a gash above his ear where his head had hit the concrete, and his lip and nose were both bleeding from the punches he'd sustained. I grabbed his face in my hands, my tears falling to mix with his blood as I cried, "No, no, no. Seth? Are you okay? Seth? Please wake up. Seth!"

Behind me, Victor was telling his men to tie Seth's hands and feet before directing his attention to me.

"Danielle, we need to go. I've already lost quite a bit of time trying to find you, and we've got to get in the air. It's too dangerous for us to stay here any longer."

Anger long pent-up exploded within me and overtook my fear.

"Go?" I asked, turning to stand and face Victor, my fists clenched at my side. "I'm not going anywhere with you. How dare you even think I would!"

"I understand that you're upset, and you have every right to be. I know I have a lot of explaining to do and a lot to make up for, and I'm committed to doing that. We can discuss whatever you need us to, but those conversations will need to take place later. Right now, I have to get you out of here and take you somewhere you can be safe."

"Safe? With you? Did you honestly think I would run into your arms like you're some knight in shining armor who's come to rescue me? You're the villain here. You're the one who put me in danger."

He frowned and arched an eyebrow. "You think I don't know that? You think I don't regret that every minute of every day?"

"Like you regret the lives you've taken? How many? How many, Vic? How many people have you killed?"

He looked away from me and closed his eyes briefly as he tapped his index knuckle against his chin. "Gentlemen, please leave me with my wife for a moment."

I glanced over my shoulder to see that the men had moved Seth to the corner on the other side of the air conditioning unit and secured his hands and feet with zip ties. He still made no movement or sound, but the slow rise and fall of his chest gave me reassurance that he was alive——for the moment, at least.

"Should we take him with us?" The taller of the two men nudged the toe of his boot roughly against Seth's hip.

"No! Stop it. Don't touch him." I moved to go back to Seth, but the third man, the one who'd held his knee in my back, stepped between us to block me, his stance wide and formidable. I whirled to face Victor. "He needs medical attention. He needs a doctor. Let me take him to a hospital."

Victor stared at me through dark eyes fringed with thick, black lashes—the same dark eyes that could have made me melt with just a glance before I knew what he was.

He hesitated, watching me intently, and I thought perhaps he might be considering my request, but then with a slight shake of his head, he'd answered his men and me, and they left us alone in the room with an unconscious Seth.

My first instinct when they were gone was to lunge at Victor, to claw at his eyes and pound on his heartless chest with all the rage I felt for him in that moment, but I refrained, knowing I must tread carefully if I was to keep Seth alive.

Victor expected my anger and would tolerate it to a point, but something told me if I went too far, the tide would turn against me, and then both Seth and I would be expendable. The only way I could save Seth was to keep Victor on my side.

He moved past me to sit on the foot of the bed, effectively blocking me from the door and from Seth. He crossed his ankle over his knee, resting his hands on his calf in a position I'd seen him assume almost daily in our brief time together, but under the present circumstances, it seemed impossibly casual. How the hell was he so calm? So collected?

It wasn't just his demeanor that seemed not to fit. His impeccable clothes, expensive shoes, and diamond-encrusted watch looked terribly out of place in the shabby surroundings. How was it possible this man had just left prison hours earlier?

Pulling a cigarillo from a case in his pocket, he bit down on it and held it in his mouth but didn't light it, perhaps honoring my request when we'd first met that he not smoke in my presence.

"I must admit my pride is a bit wounded," he said as he looked up at me. "I knew you'd be upset. I expected that. But I thought you might be at least a tiny bit happy to see me. Have you forgotten all we shared, sweetness?"

Despite my intention to use caution, my anger spewed forth again. "Don't call me that. You took everything that was sweet about us and made it bitter and acrid. What we shared was a lie. I don't even know who you are."

"Oh, but you do," he said, pulling the cigarillo from his mouth to twist it between his finger and his thumb. "Better than anyone. I was myself with you, in ways I'd never been able to be with anyone else. It was you who taught me what I wanted out of life, and what I didn't want."

"Yeah, well, it was you who taught me that I can't trust anyone and that cold-blooded murderers can pretend to be nice guys."

"It wasn't pretend," he said, his eyes softening. "You brought out the best in me, and who I was with you is who I'm meant to be. I'd never experienced love like I have with you, and I was willing—*am* willing—to risk everything for you. For us."

A time existed when those words from him would have moved me to tears and caused me to make decisions that were completely reckless and out of character. Like marrying a stranger two weeks after meeting him. But no longer.

"There is no us."

"If you will just let me explain—"

"There's nothing to explain, Victor. You kill people. Nothing you say will explain that. You're a criminal. A liar and a fraud. I only wish you'd explained all that to me when we first met. No, you know what? I wish we'd never met."

He flinched as though I'd hit him, and the pain in his eyes seemed genuine, but I felt no pity or remorse. My stomach roiled again, and I tried to remind myself to remain calm and not push him too far for Seth's sake.

"God, don't say that," he said, his voice soft and tender. "Meeting you was the best thing that has ever happened to me. You changed me. Because of you, I've turned my back on my family, my career, my life as I knew it."

"Well, because of you, my life is in danger right now. I lost my career, my life savings, and a home that I loved. I'm ashamed to look my parents in the eye, and one of the most decent men I've ever known in my life is lying over there unconscious and in need of medical attention he can't get, all because of you."

He looked down at his hands. "You're right. I can't argue any of that, nor will I try to." His eyes met mine, and for a brief second, the tenderness in them tugged at me like a memory I couldn't shake. "Danielle, I take full responsibility for my actions and for my dishonesty. I will do everything in my power to make this up to you. In our new life together, I will tell you the truth without fail from here on out. I will abide by the law, and I will restore everything you've lost and keep you safe."

"And how would you do that, Victor? Even if I could set aside everything I know and everything you've done—which I can't—do you honestly think I'd just take off and live on the run with you? Be hunted down the rest of my life?"

"You wouldn't be hunted down. I made a deal with the feds. I turned for you. I gave them what they wanted, and in exchange, I get to leave the country and live out my life as a free man. I'm asking you to come with me."

My mind spun with his words as rage shook me. I couldn't believe I'd ever found him attractive.

"You think I would just leave my family, my home, my country, and everything I've ever known in my life to be with *you*? Are you insane? Why would I do that?"

"What about the vows we made? Huh? We pledged to spend our lives together. Does that mean nothing to you?"

My mouth dropped open in disbelief. "Are you delusional? Your entire life was a lie when you stood there saying those vows to me. Does *that* mean nothing to *you?*"

"I meant every word I said in those vows. I love you. I honor you. I cherish you."

"There's no way you could honor me while hiding what you did. You have no honor."

He stood, his jaw suddenly tight and his eyes flashing anger, and I took a step back, reminded of how precarious my situation was.

"From the moment I met you, I tried to get out," he said through clenched teeth. "I did everything I could to sever ties and find a way to be with you. To be the man I was when we were together. That's *me*, Danielle." He pounded his finger against his chest. "That's the real me. The man you fell in love with is who I am in here."

He took a step toward me, and I took another step back. He noticed and retreated with his hands held up in surrender, his voice raw and breaking when he spoke.

"You think I had a choice in who I was? I was born into that life. Everyone I knew lived that life. My father, my uncles, my cousins. It was how I was raised; it was all I knew. There was no other option for me, don't you see? You don't get to decide what you want to be in a family like mine."

I shook my head. "It doesn't make it right. And it doesn't excuse you for dragging me into that life unknowingly. Unwittingly. You presented a lie to me. You allowed me to fall in love with that lie. To *marry* that lie. You had all the information, and you withheld it. I knew nothing about that life."

He exhaled slowly, and I knew he was exerting great effort to remain calm. "I didn't want you to know anything about that life. I didn't want you to know that side of me. I wanted to protect you from it."

"Well, you failed."

"I know. And I'm sorry, sweetness. I really, truly am. We can still make this work, though. We can leave, right now, and we can figure it all out."

"I don't trust you. I can't believe anything you say. I don't even know if you're telling the truth now. If you made a deal with the feds, why are you traveling with goons who beat people up?"

"First of all, they acted in your defense. We had no way of knowing who this man was or why he was at your door. But as to why they're with me, these are the men closest to me. We grew up together. They're loyal to me, not my uncle or the family. They turned with me, and for that, I'll protect them and provide for them."

"And you expect me to believe the feds just let you out of prison and gave you a plane so you and your closest friends could fly down to Florida to pick me up? That makes no sense."

Seth moaned, and I tried to go to him, but Victor blocked me, stepping to the corner of the bed to stare down at Seth.

"Who is this cop to you?" Victor asked, looking back at me. "Why are you so concerned about his health?"

"Why does he have to be someone special for me to be concerned about his health?" I asked, fearing what Victor might do if he knew who Seth was and what he meant to me. "He's a human being, and I value life. Something evidently we don't have in common."

"You called him Seth earlier," Victor said, his eyes narrowing as he put the pieces together. "Is this the infamous Seth? The one you left behind?"

My eyes must have betrayed the truth because he gave a quick nod and then looked at Seth.

"Are the two of you together then? Did you go running back to him when we fell apart?"

A sinister quality had crept into his voice, and I knew I needed to get him on the defensive again. To get him back to pleading.

"No. You called and told me my life was in danger, and I was scared. I had a choice of running alone or being with someone I trusted to protect me."

He turned his head slowly to look back at me, and I shivered at the coldness in his stare.

Had I really pledged my life to this man? Had I really thought we had a love unlike any other? How had I gotten so swept up in the whirlwind of passion and romance that I'd been unable to see his true colors?

Every instinct I'd had then had told me he was the one, but every instinct now warned me that I was in danger, and he wasn't to be trusted.

He glanced at his watch and frowned. "Unfortunately, we'll need to continue this discussion on the way to the plane. The two of you have cost me quite a bit of time on this little goose chase to find you, and we've fallen behind schedule. I'll arrange for medical help for your friend as soon as we're gone."

A nagging question stood out in the maelstrom of my mind, and I asked even though I feared the answer would only make things worse.

"How did you find me? How did you know where I was?"

"He has a tracker on your car," Seth said, his voice so thick it was almost a groan.

"Oh, my God! Seth, are you okay?" I pushed past Victor and knelt at Seth's side, not even caring about the consequences. "Are you all right?"

He ignored my questions as he tried to push himself up to sitting, which was nearly impossible given the way his hands and feet were tied. "No one followed us, and your cell phone was off. The only way he could have found you is if he was tracking your car." He took in a ragged breath and released it with a grunt that turned into a cough. "He's probably been tracking you this whole time. Watching you."

I turned to face Victor, who stood at the foot of the bed staring at me.

"Is this true? Do you have a tracker on my car?"

"My actions had put your life in danger," Victor said calmly and without emotion. "I had to do what I could to protect you, to keep you safe."

The anger returned as I stood. "So, you've had people tracking me? Watching me? My God, when does this nightmare end?"

"Your importance to me made you important to others, and knowing there were other operatives at play, I put measures in place to ensure your safety. If the order was given to make a move on you, I needed to defend you against that order or at the very least, warn you about it, as I did earlier tonight. It was for your protection, sweetness."

"She's asked you not to call her that," Seth said, and I marveled at his ability to speak with an authoritative tone as he sat hunched to one side with his hands and feet tied together.

Victor looked past me to Seth with a polite smile, but his eyes flashed with anger. "While I certainly appreciate the time and effort you put into keeping Danielle safe tonight, I'd also appreciate you butting out of what is a private conversation between me and my wife."

"Ex-wife," Seth and I both said in unison, and Victor's jaw muscle flexed in response.

His phone rang in his pocket, and he stared at me through two full rings before he reached for it. "I have to take this, and then we have to go."

The warm, pleading supplication in his voice was completely gone, replaced by a dispassionate and commanding matter-of-fact tone that sent a chill down my spine.

Time was running out.

TEN

V ictor walked toward the vanity on the other side of the room as he took the call, and I knelt by Seth again, my tears coming so quickly I had no time to block them.

"I'm so sorry," I cried in a whisper.

"I'm the one who should apologize," Seth whispered back. "I said I'd protect you, and I failed."

"No, it's my fault. I never should have dragged you into this, and I'm going to get you out of it, I promise. Victor said if I go with him, he'll send you medical help."

"No," Seth growled. "Don't you dare leave with him."

"I have to. It's the only way I know they won't harm you."

"That's ridiculous. You going won't stop them from doing whatever they're gonna do to me. It only puts you in more danger."

My tears gushed forth as I struggled to keep my voice down. I glanced back at Victor, who was still on the phone and speaking in a hushed, but angry, voice. "He made a deal with the feds, which means he can't kill you, right? He said he can leave the country safely and if I go—"

"Listen to me. He didn't make any damned deal, and you know

that as well as I do, or you wouldn't be worried about me. If I don't call Tristan in the next few minutes to check in, he's going to swarm this place. You just have to stall. Keep them here, okay? Don't leave with him, babe. Promise me?"

"We can't wait any longer," Victor said as he walked back toward us. "We have to go."

"And you'll get him help, right? You'll call an ambulance for him?"

With a brief nod, Victor shoved his hands in his pockets. "He'll be seen to once we're clear of the area."

"Why can't you call for help now?" I wiped my tears away with the back of my hand and stood to go to Victor, willing to plead, to beg, to do anything to ensure Seth would be safe. "He helped me out tonight, Vic. We can't just leave him here bleeding. Please, let's cut the zip ties and call a doctor before we go, okay?"

When I got no response, I moved closer, sliding my arms up his chest and around his neck, ignoring the repulsion in my gut. He stood staring down at me, unmoving and with no discernible emotion in his eyes.

Trying my hardest to be convincing, I softened my voice and leaned in. "This has all been a lot to process, Vic. I need time to wrap my head around everything. I'm willing to go with you. I'll listen to what you have to say, and I'll try to forgive you, but I'm asking this one thing from you first. I'll have enough guilt leaving my family behind, won't I? I can't abandon my oldest friend and walk away without knowing he'll be all right. Surely, if the feds allowed you to come all the way to Florida to get me, they can wait a few minutes longer until we know Seth gets the help he needs."

He still didn't react, so I molded my body to him, moving my hands to the back of his neck as I stretched up on my tiptoes to press my lips against his.

For what seemed like an eternity but was likely only seconds, he remained still as a stone statue, but then something primal kicked in, and with a deep guttural moan, his mouth began to ravage mine as he twisted his hands in my hair and then moved them up and down my body like a man starved of physical touch. I fought with myself to allow him to continue, and bile rose in my throat as his tongue plundered me and his lips bruised mine.

"God, I've missed you, sweetness," he murmured as he moved to bury his face in my neck, sucking and nibbling at my skin. His hands cupped my buttocks, lifting me against his hardness and damned near making me vomit. "It's been so long."

Seth coughed behind me, and I couldn't hold the ruse any longer.

I tried to wriggle free of Victor's grasp but didn't dare look at Seth.

"I missed you, too," I said, breathless from my efforts not to scream or puke. "But let's not lose our focus. You said we need to get going. Let me call someone to come help Seth, and we'll be on our way."

Victor was breathless, too, his eyes dark with desire and his lips swollen. He held onto my hips with both hands, unwilling to let me go completely, and I watched as the desire became veiled with suspicion.

"Are you playing me, my love?" He reached to trace his thumb across my bottom lip, gently at first, but then rougher as he pushed it inside my mouth. He swiped it across my tongue and then moved it to his own mouth, sucking at my saliva before pulling his thumb free from his lips with a loud pop. "That could be both cruel and dangerous. To take a man who's been locked up for two years, deprived of the one thing he desires most, and then dangle it in front of him."

Memories of our bodies entangled flashed unwanted in my mind, and I shuddered at the thought of how intimately he knew me and how unclean that made me feel.

"Maybe she's just concerned for your safety," Seth said. "And her own. You've been ranting all night that her life's in danger and that you need to go, so she might like to be somewhere safer for this little reunion. Or perhaps it's modesty. I never knew her to be one who wanted an audience when we were together."

Victor stiffened at Seth's reference, and I wanted to throttle Seth for stoking Vic's anger when it was so imperative to keep it at bay.

"Hey," I said, laying my hand along Victor's cheek as I pressed myself against him again. "You boys can trade barbs back and forth if you want, but you're wasting time that we don't have." I brushed my lips softly against his. "I'm still angry with you, you know? You can't think I'm just gonna hop right back into bed with you in the first ten minutes. You said you'd make all this up to me, and I expect you to at least make an effort at it before I give myself to you again."

The words felt vile in my mouth, but they seemed to placate him, and he kissed me again, more tenderly this time.

Seth cleared his throat behind us. "Hey, I hate to interrupt such a tender moment, but I was just thinking that it might go a long way to ease her fears and help her trust you if she could verify what you're saying. I mean, if you made a deal with the feds, then that should be something she could confirm, right?"

Victor pulled away from our kiss and directed his gaze at Seth. "Arrangements at the highest levels aren't made public knowledge, but I'm certain you knew that when you made your suggestion."

"Maybe not public knowledge, but it could likely be verified by a well-connected law enforcement officer."

"Meaning you?" Victor said with a smirk.

"No, I'm just a lowly deputy, but I know people who would be able to verify this sort of thing. You know, to put Dani's mind at ease. If you'd untie me and return my phone, I'd be happy to make that call for the two of you. Seeing as how you and your friends are here with legitimate permission, it shouldn't pose any risk to untie me and let me make a call, right?"

I knew Seth was trying to stall, doing whatever he could to goad Victor and delay our departure, but I feared his plan would backfire. Seth was only alive because Victor wanted to convince me he had changed. If Seth pushed him too far, then Victor might decide it didn't matter what I thought, in which case, Seth and I both would be in far greater danger.

Victor released me and walked over to stand in front of Seth. "If there's anything I've learned about law enforcement officers from my time outside and inside a prison cell, it's that anyone can be bought for a price. I have no way of knowing who you're truly working for, and having just gotten my future back, I don't intend to trade it away so soon. Especially not by trusting someone with an obvious vendetta."

"Vendetta? What do you mean?" I asked, moving myself between the two men.

"Don't you see, sweetness?" Victor smiled as he spoke to me, but his eyes never left Seth's. "We're dealing with a man scorned. You left him all those years ago, and I got the prize he'd been denied. He's never had the honor of calling you his wife. You told me how he tried for months to reach you after you severed all ties. He was unwilling to let you go, and of course, I can understand why. I'm certainly not willing to give up, but then again, I know better than he what I stand to lose. You did tell me, did you not, that the passion and sexual chemistry we shared made your past experiences pale in comparison."

I looked back at Seth with an apologetic frown as Victor twisted my words into a dagger to plunge into Seth's pride, but his bloodied and swollen face showed no reaction at all.

"Stop," I said to Victor. "You're being cruel, and I don't appreciate you using me as a pawn to hurt someone."

"It's okay," Seth said. "I understand why he wants to make this about me. If I'd screwed up as badly as he has, if I'd lied to you and betrayed you on that level, I'm sure I'd want to deflect attention away from myself too."

A rap at the door startled me, and I turned as Victor called out, "You have the key, don't you? Come in."

The man who'd held his knee in my back entered and gave Seth's phone to Victor. "It's lighting up with texts. I guess he was supposed to call somebody and missed the time frame."

Victor scanned the text conversation and then looked at Seth.

"Well, haven't you been the busy one this evening?" He turned to the man and nodded. "We're about to have company. Have Nicholas pull around front. Paulie can drive her car with him," he said, nodding toward Seth. "Danielle will ride with me."

"No!" I protested, my panic rising. "You said you'd leave Seth here. That you'd get him help. If you have a deal with the feds, then what does it matter if the cops come? You can just tell them, right? You tell them that you have a deal, and they'll let you go. I mean, um, they'll let *us* go."

"I'm sorry, Danielle," Victor said. "It doesn't work that way. The deal I made was for me to disappear. My name and my dealings with the federals can't be revealed to anyone. You have to understand what lengths I've gone to just to be with you, my love. I've exposed immensely powerful people who would kill to get their hands on me, literally, and if we alert members of law enforcement, well, then we risk a paid member of the force selling us out."

"He's right, Dani," Seth said. "Which is why he should untie me and let me drive you to the plane."

"You're delusional if you think that's happening," Victor sneered.

"Maybe I am, but you need to hear me out. Any minute now, my colleagues are going to descend on this hotel. One call from me and I could stop that from happening. I tell my partner that I fell asleep. Didn't hear his texts or calls. I tell him Dani and I are fine, and that we're going to hit the road again. The imminent threat from law enforcement goes away, and you make your way to the plane. Dani can meet you there."

Victor stared at Seth with narrowed eyes as he tapped his fingers on the edge of Seth's phone. "Let's say you did this, and let's say it worked. Why on earth would I allow you to drive away from here with my wife?"

"You yourself just pointed out the ruthless people who are after you. It's imperative that you get on that plane and in the air before they locate you. But you've been delayed, and that bought them time. If they find you, and Dani's with you, we both know she won't make it out of that alive, and God only knows what might happen to her before death comes."

I flinched at his casual mention of my death and refused to think of what could precede it.

"On the flip side," Seth continued, "thanks to my raising alarms this evening, you've got local law enforcement on the lookout too, and even if I make the call that we're leaving the motel, they'll still be looking for you. If they catch you, they think you're an escaped convict, and as you explained, you can't tell them otherwise. If Dani's with you when you get caught, she's an accessory. She gets locked up, too. So, the only way to keep her safe is through me. Let me take her and we'll meet up with you."

Victor lifted an eyebrow, and one side of his mouth curled. "Considering that you're tied up and without your gun, your badge, or your phone, I'd say you didn't do a particularly good job of protecting Danielle when you had the opportunity. Why would I ever trust that which I hold most precious in my heart to you when you've already failed? Enough talk. Danielle, we must go."

"Have you asked her if she wants to go?" Seth asked, his words tumbling out in a rush in his desperation to stall the inevitable. "You keep telling her what she *must* do, what she has to do, but what about what she wants? Is she able to decide for herself? If you're forcing her to go with you, then it's not love; it's kidnapping. Do you love her enough to set her free? Or will you make her go? Take her against her will?"

I held my breath as I waited for Victor's reaction. While I understood what Seth was doing and couldn't help but appreciate his efforts, I also feared he was going to push us all past the point of no return. I didn't know what Victor would do if I refused to go. I didn't want to believe he would harm me or take me by force, but I hadn't wanted to believe he was a killer either, and I'd been wrong about that.

If Seth forced Victor's hand and the pretense of my free will was dropped, then I became Victor's prisoner and there would be nothing to stop him from ordering Seth's death. I refused to let things reach that point if I could stop it. As long as we all pretended I was willing, Seth had a chance.

"Thanks for looking out for me, Seth, but I already told Victor I'm willing to go with him. I think I should at least give him a chance to explain his side of the story." I turned to look at Victor. "Of course, I assume if things don't work out between us, I'll be free to come back home."

"Of course," Victor said, his murderous gaze toward Seth softening as he shifted it to look at me. "I would never hold you against your will." He took my hand and lifted it to his lips, planting a soft kiss there before smiling at me.

Ned knocked but twisted the key in the lock and entered without waiting for an invitation. "Ready, boss?"

"Yes. Ned, gather my wife's belongings."

"What about Seth?" I asked. "You said we'd call for medical attention."

Victor placed his hand in the small of my back and nudged me toward the door. "And we will, once we're clear of the area."

"At least untie him!"

His nudge grew more firm and when I still didn't budge, he put his arm around me and sighed.

"Danielle, I do not trust this man. He carries a torch for you, and he would like nothing more than to remove me from the situation to better his chances. He remains under restraint until we're gone."

I cast a glance over my shoulder at Seth as I allowed Victor to guide me out the door behind Ned.

Seth had begun to fight against his restraints like a mad man. "Don't go with him! Dani, please!"

His voice echoed in my ears as the door closed, and I could still hear him as I climbed into the back seat of a black SUV. I started to scoot across, expecting Victor to join me, but he held tight to my hand and then leaned forward to kiss me. I pulled back as soon as our lips met.

"What are you doing?" I asked. "Aren't you coming with me?"

"Your friend was right. It puts you in more danger to travel with me. My men will protect you and bring you to me."

"No, wait," I said, even more panicked at the thought of being alone with the two strangers. "I want to come with you."

"We won't be parted long, my love."

Releasing my hand, he nodded to Ned in the front passenger seat and then closed the door, and the driver, a man I hadn't seen before, sped away with me. I looked back, relieved to see Victor climb into the other SUV. I'd feared he might go back in the room to harm Seth, but it appeared he'd kept his word. My sacrifice had been worth it so far. Seth was alive, and with Tristan arriving soon, hopefully, they'd be able to find me before it was too late.

ELEVEN

The bars in the area were closing, which made traffic heavier than I'd expected for the wee hours of the morning.

Each time we stopped for a red light, I tried to make eye contact with the people in the cars next to us, hoping to send a silent distress signal, but no one even bothered to look my direction. Not that they would have been able to see me through the dark tinted windows, anyway.

With Seth no longer in immediate danger, my mind shifted to considering my own fate. The full ramifications of my situation came crashing down like a weight on my chest, and my lungs struggled to expand for a full breath as I second-guessed my decision and began to search for an escape.

I looked behind us, surprised to see that the other SUV wasn't there.

"Where's Victor?"

"They went a different route so we wouldn't be together if something went wrong," Ned said, glancing back at me. "Don't worry. We'll be meeting up with him in just a few minutes."

Which meant I only had a few minutes to save myself from this situation.

We were almost out of the populated area, and one last convenience store could be seen up ahead on the right.

"I need to use the restroom," I said. "Could we stop at that store?"

Ned groaned, his irritation evident.

"No way. We've had enough delays. We keep driving."

"It will only take a minute," I said, leaning forward to look at Ned.

"Boss said to bring you straight to him. That's what we're doing."

"You realize I'm free to go wherever I'd like, right? Victor's not forcing me to join him; that's my choice. So, you're here to protect me, not confine me. Pull over at that store, so I can use the bathroom."

Ned gave me a look that made it clear he didn't agree with my concept of freedom, but he motioned for the driver to pull into the store's parking lot.

I'd been hoping there would be plenty of witnesses so I could make a big scene and demand that someone call the police without Ned being able to stop me, but to my dismay, only one other car was there, and it was parked around on the side of the store. Maybe even the lone employee's car for all I knew.

Reaching for the door handle to get out, alarmed to find the child-lock engaged.

"Can you unlock my door, please?"

Ned got out and opened the door for me, and then he began to follow me inside.

"What are you doing?" I asked, whirling to face him.

"I'm going in with you."

"I think I can go pee by myself. There's no one here, and if someone does come, you'll see them from out here and be able to stop them, won't you?"

"I'm not letting you go in there alone."

I scoffed and crossed my arms. "Again, Ned, with all due respect to you trying to do your job, I'm not being held captive here. I can go to the bathroom without an audience."

He hesitated, and then he cursed and pulled his phone from his pocket. "Make this quick. I need to call the boss and let him know we've stopped."

"Be my guest." As soon as I was inside the store, I walked toward the restrooms in the back but then ducked into the last aisle and crouched so Ned couldn't see me. I maneuvered into a position where I could see the clerk and began to plead with him. "I need to use your phone, please. It's an emergency."

He stared at me from behind his plexiglass haven. "We don't have a phone for customers to use."

I stood up enough to peer over the shelves and check for Ned's location but was unable to see out with all the posters on the windows. "It's an emergency! Please," I said as I crouched back down.

"I'm sorry. I'm not allowed to let you use the phone."

"Then, here, can you call someone for me?" I reached into my pocket and pulled out the folded piece of paper where Seth had written Tristan's number earlier. "I'll read off the number to you and you can call and let this person know where I am."

"I'm sorry," he said again and moved out of my sight line. "I don't want to get involved."

A cell phone rang in the back of the store, and I ran toward the sound. It was coming from the men's bathroom, and I pounded on the door as I yelled, "Hello? I need to use your phone, please. It's an emergency."

I pressed my ear to the door, waiting for a response. A muffled male voice was talking inside, and I ran back down the short hallway to see if Ned had come in yet. After confirming the store was still empty, I went and pounded on the door of the men's room again.

"Hello? Please, I need your phone. It's an emergency. Please hurry."

"All right, I'm coming," said a voice from inside, and I backed away from the door and listened as water ran and then shut off.

The lock turned and the door opened, and I stood there frozen as Metro Man smiled at me.

"Well, hello, Danielle," he said with a wicked grin, and he lunged for me as I turned to run.

He grabbed me from behind, pinning my arms against my ribs and lifting me off the ground. Instead of walking back toward the store, he carried me screaming in the direction of the door at the end of the hallway. I had only my feet and legs to use as weapons, and I kicked at the boxes lining the hall, knocking them into his path. He adjusted his grip with a loud swear and twisted me to the side so he could see in front of him.

Given his slim build, his strength surprised me, and I found it hard to breathe as he tightened his hold and forced air from my lungs. As we came to the door, he had to loosen his grip to reach for the knob, and I was able to pull one arm free. I began pounding at his other arm and at his face, and then when that didn't deter him, I reached up and behind me to grab a handful of his long hair, jerking at it and causing his man bun to come undone.

He cursed as he placed his hand over mine and fought to free his hair, never slowing in his progress across the storage room toward another door. I held onto his hair as long as I could, but as he continued to apply more pressure in crushing my hand beneath his, eventually my pain threshold was reached. I let go, and he grabbed my wrist and wrenched my arm behind my back, my fingers still holding the strands of his hair I'd pulled out. I kicked at his shins and did my best to butt his head with mine as we got closer to the door, but then he placed me in a chokehold with my arm pinned between us, and everything went black in seconds.

When I came to, I was being shoved into the back seat of a car, my hands pulled behind me and secured tightly with something that felt as though it was cutting into my skin.

A burly man with black hair and a black beard climbed into the back seat behind me, and Metro Man got into the driver's seat and started the car as I kicked and screamed.

"Tie her damned feet so she stops that kicking," Metro Man said.

"You sure that's okay?" Burly Man asked. "We're supposed to deliver her unharmed."

"Yeah, well, she's gonna harm herself kicking like that, and if she doesn't stop, I'm willing to harm her and take the consequences."

Burly Man pulled a zip tie from his pocket, and I kicked at him even harder, doing all I could to prevent him from grabbing my feet, but despite my best efforts, I was no match for his size and brute strength.

Once I'd been restrained, my mind tried to catch up with the newest turn of events. I'd only thought I was scared before when I was in the car with killers I sort of knew via Victor. I'd at least had some confidence they wouldn't harm me out of respect for their boss. These killers were unknown, and that unleashed a whole new level of fear.

Who were these men and where were they taking me? I tried to take comfort in knowing whoever their boss was had instructed them not to harm me, but it gave me no assurances of how I would fare once I reached our destination, especially since Metro Man seemed all too willing to disobey that order before we even got there.

Was it possible Ned had heard me scream? Even if he hadn't, I knew he'd come inside the store looking for me once I didn't return, but would that asshat of a clerk be able to tell him anything? When Metro Man shoved me in his car, it was parked behind the store. Had he entered the same way? If so, would the clerk even be able to describe him to Ned? How would Ned find me?

I couldn't believe my situation had become so dire that I was hoping for Ned the Gangster to be my savior.

As I replayed the harrowing scene in my head, I realized Metro Man hadn't looked particularly surprised to see me when he opened the door of the men's room. In fact, he'd looked as though he expected me and was ready to pounce.

We had stopped at the store randomly, so there's no way he was lying in wait, but he'd been on the phone seconds before he saw me. Had someone called to tip him off? Had someone watched me go in the store?

It was highly possible the Mafia had tracked Victor to the motel and then watched us all leave. Had I been thrown from the frying pan into the fire, now facing an even worse fate than the one I'd been considering earlier?

"Where are you taking me?" I asked, but neither of the men answered. "You're making a big mistake. There will be people looking for me, powerful people. They will hunt you down."

"See if you can gag her, would ya?" Metro Man said. "Shut her up."

Burly Man snorted. "You might be willing to take the consequences, but I'm not."

I tried to decipher landmarks as we drove through the darkness, but my unfamiliarity with the area made it impossible to determine where we were or where we might be going.

My throat burned from screaming, and my ribs ached from fighting against Metro Man's grip. A searing pain throbbed in my right shoulder from the violent twisting of my arm behind my back, and sitting with my hands restrained behind me didn't help it any. My wrists stung from the sharp edges of what I assumed was a zip tie holding them together, and only by sitting very still could I keep my ankles from suffering the same fate.

I had so many questions, but I didn't dare ask them. Metro Man didn't seem like the kind of guy who made empty threats, and since I had no desire to be gagged, I maintained silence for the rest of our journey.

He glanced back at me once we'd left the streetlights behind and entered a rural area with dark trees lining both sides of the road. "How are you doing back there? You sure do have a lot of sass. I've often wondered as I watched you these past few months what kind of spitfire you might be if you were provoked, and you didn't disappoint."

My mind reeled at the implication of his revelations. I'd only seen him for the first time in the grocery store a week earlier, but if he'd been watching me for months, where else had he been that I hadn't known about?

Our eyes met in the rearview mirror, and he grinned broadly, obviously pleased with my distress.

"Of course, I knew when I discovered you were a straight-up whiskey girl that you'd be tough. Oh, and sorry about that bottle at the theater. I was awful thirsty that night."

I sucked in a gasp of air as a puzzle piece locked into place. I'd left a full whiskey bottle at the theater one night while working there, and when I returned the next morning, the bottle had been empty. The foreman had been outraged when I'd outright accused his workers of drinking it, and even after his assurances of their innocence, I'd always harbored a resentment and wondered which of the men was a liar and a thief.

Knowing the truth only made things worse. My stomach felt as though it might flip inside out to consider that Metro Man had been inside my building. Had he been in my house as well?

"How about you be the one who shuts up now?" Burly Man said, bumping his knee against the back of Metro Man's seat. "You're doing no one any good running your mouth like this."

"What harm does it do? I never laid a hand on her. I must admit, I had a bit of fun screwing with her head, though." His eyes met mine again in the mirror, and I looked away, unwilling to let him see my fear. "You thought you were going nuts, didn't you? Nope. That was me moving your hairbrush from the bathroom to the living room sofa. Switching around the flowerpots on the front porch just to see if I could make you pause and notice when you came home at night. Leaving the creamer out on your kitchen counter. And why'd you switch to the hazelnut? I much preferred the French vanilla."

I shut my eyes and swallowed down the nausea that overcame

me. The confirmation that I hadn't been crazy about all these little things gave me no comfort. Instead, I felt violated. Exposed. Threatened.

"You're nuts," Burly Man told him. "You were supposed to be discreet. Unseen. You're lucky you didn't get caught."

"I had to do something to pass the time in that boring ass town. I felt like I'd been banished to the ends of the earth with this assignment. Luckily, Danielle was beautiful and easy to watch."

Opening my eyes, I glared at him, wishing my hatred and anger could somehow set him ablaze. Instead, he chuckled and reached to adjust the rearview mirror to make it easier for him to look me in the eye.

"I enjoyed my view immensely. Tell me, though. How long did you search for that silky red nightie you were sure you'd tossed across the chair in your bedroom? It smelled so damned lovely I had to take it home with me."

Burly Man clucked his tongue against his teeth. "Better not let anyone else hear you say that. You only thought you'd been banished before. They find out you were screwing around and playing games or getting some kind of personal pleasure out of this, you're done for."

"No harm was done, was it, Danielle?" He winked at me in the mirror, and I looked away again. "I even bought her a round at the bar to make up for the whiskey I drank. I always pay my debts. And then tonight, karma rewarded me, and you fell into my arms. Would you believe I worked at that shithole of a store when I was a teenager? They still don't lock the back door. Makes it easier for the night cashier to sneak out back and meet a friend for a smoke."

He slowed the car and turned right into a gated neighborhood. My hopes rose when I saw a guarded entrance, but then Metro Man took to the far-right lane and a gate opened without him needing to get clearance, squashing any opportunity for me to scream for help.

As we wound around through the neighborhood, each house grew larger and more grandiose than the last. Any one of them could be considered an estate on its own with large sloping yards and winding driveways. The deeper in we went, the more mature the trees were and the farther off the road the houses were set, and soon, the homes weren't even visible in the darkness, their presence only indicated by the occasional driveway gate and the distant flickering of lights behind the trees.

The road seemed to stretch forever ahead of us, and I marveled at the massive size of the neighborhood. For the most part, there had been few walls or fences marking the property lines, but after rounding a wide curve, we came upon a stone wall at least ten feet high that ran alongside the right edge of the road. Once we'd reached its driveway, the wall curved back from the road leading to massive wrought iron gates set between two stone pillars that looked like castle bastions. Metro Man pulled into the drive and then stopped the car as two men dressed in black and carrying huge black guns stepped forward in front of the gate.

The men separated and walked down each side of the car, their guns pointed at us, and I held my breath, fearful the sound of bullets might pierce the air as Metro Man opened his window and leaned out with a little wave.

"We've got a package for delivery. We're expected."

The men outside the car nodded to each other and then one of them did some sort of signal with his arm, and the gate began to swing open.

As we moved through the enormous gates, any hope left in my heart dissipated. Tristan had probably stormed the hotel by now and found Seth. Seth would have been able to bring him up to speed, and they would have set out looking for me with a description of Victor and his men, hitting all the area's airstrips first since Seth knew Victor intended to fly.

But even if they found Victor and stopped him from fleeing the country, they wouldn't find me. I pictured Seth's frustration and agony when he discovered I was no longer with Victor, and for the first time since Metro Man had taken me as his captive, I imagined what Victor's reaction might be to losing me after going to such lengths to get me back.

Would Victor know who these people were? Would he come for me in some ill-fated rescue attempt? Or after everything that had transpired, would he cut his losses and leave without me, choosing freedom over his misguided notion of love?

The driveway meandered through the woods, the pitch-black darkness dotted with low lights on either side of the road every hundred feet or so. With every twist and turn of the drive, my heart sank further and my hopes for escape diminished. Even if I found a way out of wherever they were taking me and managed to make my way back to the road without being caught, how the hell would I scale that wall?

Eventually, we came into a clearing, at the back of which sat the largest house I'd ever seen, and that was based only on what was illuminated by spotlights since the rest disappeared into the night. It was literally a castle, with stone turrets and a large wooden bridge suspended by chains over a narrow moat of water. If I had been able to hold onto a shred of hope before, it would have been extinguished by this formidable fortress. I wondered if it had been built to keep its inhabitants safe or to keep them from escaping.

Metro Man drove us over the wooden bridge and beneath the tall archway that led to a graveled central courtyard. The building surrounded us on all sides, and two men stood sentry on either side of the double doors at the center of the wall facing us.

They moved forward as Metro Man put the car in park, and then the larger of the two opened my door. I shrank back from him, recoiling when my back hit Burly Man's shoulder, and then, to my surprise, the towering hulk of a man who'd opened my door smiled at me and extended his hand as though I was a princess arriving for afternoon tea.

He frowned as he took in my restraints, and then he leaned forward to glare at Burly Man.

"Why is she tied up?"

Burly Man pointed toward Metro Man, who had already gotten out of the car and was talking with the other sentry.

"Ask him. I told him it wasn't a good idea."

Without waiting for an answer, the giant reached into his pocket and grabbed a knife, severing the zip ties and freeing my hands and feet as he mumbled something I couldn't make out.

He took my hands and examined my raw and red wrists, and then he pulled me gently from the car. His kindness caught me off-guard, and though a voice in the back of my head screamed at me to run or to at least put up a fight once I was out of the car, I did neither.

Maybe it was exhaustion from lack of sleep, lack of food, too much whiskey and too much fear, or perhaps it was common sense and the knowledge that I wouldn't get far—likely not even past the giant—but my feet followed the giant inside to find a huge foyer with two-story ceilings and a garish crystal chandelier hanging between two curving stairwells.

He called out for someone named Bea, and a short, elderly lady wearing a gray maid's uniform came through a doorway at the back of the entry hall.

"Here you are," she said, smiling wide as though she was greeting an expected guest she'd longed to see. "Let me show you to your room."

The surrealness of the environment led me to wonder if I'd been knocked unconscious and was having some sort of bizarre dream, which seemed infinitely more plausible than the Mafia being this hospitable to their kidnapping victims.

"The idiot tied her wrists," the giant said. "Can you clean them up?"

"Of course."

She held my hands to examine my wrists, her white hair close enough to my nostrils for me to smell the green apple scent of her hairspray.

"Don't worry, dear. We'll get some salve and bandages on these."

Giving my hands a tender squeeze, she released them and turned to go, and with a glance over my shoulder at the giant, I followed her.

The amount of shock I'd sustained in the past few hours had begun to overwhelm my senses, and a numbness seeped through me as I walked behind Bea up the wide wooden staircase. I knew I needed to figure out where I was, who had abducted me and why, and most importantly, how to get free, but for the moment, I was content to catch my breath. My fear hadn't lessened, but without the imminent threat of being beaten or tortured, my heart slowed its frantic pace and my thoughts became calmer and more analytical.

Physical escape seemed pretty much off the table as an option, so I would need to determine who had the potential to be an ally, and this maid with the kind smile and the green apple hair seemed like as good a place as any to start.

TWELVE

Bea turned left at the top of the stairs and led me down a wide hallway lined with doors. The third door on the right was ajar, and she stepped inside, swinging the door open wide as she turned and swept her arm toward the room to invite me in.

"Here we are," she said with a pleasant smile. "Your favorite whiskey has been placed there on the sideboard with a bucket of ice. I'm told that's how you like it. Shall I pour you some?"

What the hell? Did they treat all their kidnapping victims this well before they murdered them? "Um, no, thanks."

"Would you like a different cold beverage? Or perhaps a hot one?"

Even though I was thirsty and would have loved either the whiskey or some water, I shook my head. Given the circumstances, I didn't trust anything I might be given.

"Let me know if you change your mind," Bea said with a smile. "Now, I'll go and get some first aid supplies for your wrists and leave you to settle in."

Settle in? Her welcoming speech was more appropriate for a bed and breakfast hostess than a servant of the Mafia. Had I stepped into an alternate universe? Who were these people? Why had they taken me and what plans did they have for me? Did they mean to kill me with kindness?

Bea didn't wait for any reply on my part, which was great since I was too stunned to give her one.

As soon as she'd left the room and closed the door, I headed straight to the window and pulled back the heavy moss-colored silk drapes and the thick blind. Nothing but pitch blackness greeted me, so devoid of any light or shadow that I suspected the window had been blacked out or covered with a film.

After checking the other window and finding the same, I turned and went to the door, opening it slowly and pausing as it creaked. I peeked my head out into the hallway and looked first to the right and then to the left, and then I made my way toward the stairs, frowning when I saw the giant standing sentry by the front door.

He gave a nod of acknowledgment, and I lifted my hand in an awkward wave and then retreated back into the room and closed the door.

Despite their warm welcome, it appeared I was still a prisoner under guard. The calming numbness that had overtaken me when I'd arrived began to evaporate, and my heart resumed its frantic pace as I searched the room for a phone or anything to identify my captors. The search proved fruitless. My luxurious prison cell had every comfort one might need for a short stay but lacked any communication devices or ties to the world outside its walls.

Defeated and back to feeling hopeless, I flopped down on the chaise lounge in the corner and stared at my surroundings. The opulent room with its soft moss-greens and creamy peaches and taupes was a far cry from the motel I'd left behind. The king-sized four-poster bed had a plush tapestry duvet and eight thick, fluffy pillows stacked neatly against the headboard, and I yearned to crawl beneath the covers and shut my eyes, blocking out reality and all that came with it.

"May I come in?" Bea knocked as she said it but entered without waiting for a response. "Come and sit here on the bed, and I'll get you cleaned up."

Once again, her nonchalant and easygoing demeanor threw me off. My mind kept telling me to stay on high alert and look for any advantage or route of escape, but in Bea's comforting presence, the risk of danger seemed far removed.

Following her instruction, I moved to sit on the side the bed as she adjusted the lamp on the nightstand so its beam would shine on my wrists. She hummed as she worked, her touch gentle, and despite the obvious implications, I couldn't make my mind accept that this seemingly sweet-natured and caring person worked for the Mafia and assisted them in holding people against their will.

Yet, she must have some inkling of what was happening. After all, she hadn't shown any surprise or curiosity at a stranger being dropped off at the front door in the middle of the night, and she hadn't seemed the least bit shocked or alarmed to learn that my wrists had been secured with a zip tie. Based on her reaction when I'd arrived, she'd been expecting me. A room had been chosen and the lights turned on ahead of time with my favorite drink on hand.

What did she think was the reason for my being there? Did she know I had been kidnapped? Did it matter? Seemingly oblivious to my fear and my plight, she went about applying a thick salve to the raw spots on my wrists and then wrapping them in a thin gauze bandaging.

"Bea?" I asked when she was nearly done.

"Yes, dear?"

"I need your help," I whispered, wary of what I was doing but determined to move forward.

She looked up at me for the first time since she'd began seeing to my wrists, her blue eyes clear and framed by deep laugh lines. Surely, this lady wasn't associated with killers. She couldn't be. She was someone's grandma; I was sure of it.

I cleared my throat and blurted out the words before I lost my courage. "I've been brought here against my will."

She bent her head and went back to work on my wrists as though I'd not spoken at all.

Unwilling to give up just yet, I leaned in closer. "I need you to call someone for me."

With a tender pat on my arm, she had finished securing my bandage, and she stood upright and put her hands on her hips, surveying her handiwork. "That should do it. That salve is like a miracle cure, I tell you. You'll be surprised how much better your wrists look if you leave those bandages on for a few hours. All the redness will be gone."

As she tidied up and gathered her supplies, she began to hum again with no acknowledgment of anything I'd said.

Desperate for her help and fearing who might come once she'd left, I tried again. "Bea, please. If you could just call this number—" I reached into my pocket for Tristan's number, but the piece of paper wasn't there. Had I dropped it at the store? Had someone taken it during the brief time I was unconscious? My panic level rose, and I began to cry. "Please help me."

Wordlessly, she walked toward the door, but then she stopped and looked back at me, her hand on the knob and her eyes still just as kind as ever.

"Pull yourself together, dear, and muster some strength. They prey on weakness, and they thrive on fear. Don't let them see your backbone bend."

"Who is they?"

One eyebrow arched, and the corner of her mouth rose in a smirk. "The family, dear. You know, the one you married into. Who did you think? I suggest you get some rest. It's my understanding you won't be here long."

When she'd gone, she took with her any comfort her presence had given, and my mind raced anew with terror at the confirmation of what I suppose I'd already known. The family. The Mafia. The people Victor had betrayed. He said he'd done it for me, and now, it seemed I would be required to pay the price for my choices and his.

THIRTEEN

Lying back across the lush duvet, I covered my eyes with my arm and fought against the tears. Bea was right. I had to pull myself together. Falling apart would do me no good, and I needed to keep my wits about me. I focused on taking deep, slow breaths, and in my exhausted state, it must have worked a little too well.

I didn't know I was dreaming at first. I opened my eyes to my bedroom back in Chicago, in the house I'd loved and painstakingly restored. It was all there—everything I'd had to pack up or give away or leave behind. The tapestry I'd found at a street market hung on the wall above my antique bed. The tall, thin paper lantern sculpture from the little art gallery two blocks over sat in the corner, and the multi-colored glass chimes hanging in front of the window scattered the sun's rays across the room in rainbow prism splashes of color.

The smell of frying bacon wafted through the air, and I arched my back and stretched my arms above my head, yawning. I stood and wandered down the hall, wrapping my robe around me and tying it at the waist as I went. In my dream state, I was blissfully unaware of anything that had gone awry in the past two years, and I smiled at the thought of the day ahead with my husband.

As I neared the kitchen, I recognized the tune Victor was whistling. It was from an old black and white movie we'd watched the night before. We hadn't made it to the end. As often happened with us, we'd gotten preoccupied with passion, preferring our own love story to any other we watched.

I opened my mouth to tell him good morning as I entered the kitchen, but I stopped, my mouth and eyes both opened wide at the sight of Seth sitting at the kitchen table.

My heart leapt with joy, and I ran over and threw my arms around him. He stood, laughing as he held me tightly and spun me in a circle, and then he set me back down.

"I finally made it," he said with the smile I adored, his chocolate-brown eyes dancing with obvious delight. "It took me a while, but I'm here!"

"What do you mean?" My brow furrowed, and I cocked my head to the side, hoping it meant what I thought it did. "You're here, like you *moved* here? You came to Chicago for me?"

"Of course," Seth said. "I promised you, didn't I?"

"Oh my gosh!" I hugged him so tightly that he grunted and reached to loosen my grip around his ribs.

"I can't breathe, D," he said, laughing. "Let's go see the city. I want you to show me everything. All your favorite spots. Share it all with me."

He bent his head to kiss me, and I stretched onto my tiptoes, eager to welcome him.

"Danielle?" Victor called from behind me, and I whirled at the sound of his voice.

He stood at the oven, wearing nothing but my yellow and blue striped apron as he fried bacon and scrambled eggs.

Alarmed, I looked back and forth between them, but neither of them seemed the least bit concerned to both be in my kitchen at the same time, and neither seemed to care that Victor was practically nude.

"I'm making breakfast for you," Victor said, his smile widening.

Their physical similarities had never dawned on me, but seeing them together that way, they were almost exactly the same height, and their hair and eyes were nearly identical shades of brown, though as I looked closer, I could see Seth's irises were a tad bit lighter. They were both lean, but Seth's rigorous training had given his upper body more bulk.

"Sorry it took me so long," Seth said as he reached to brush his fingers across my brow and then twisted a lock of my hair. "Mom was sick, and Zara needed me. But I'm here now, and I always will be."

"Danielle?" Victor's smile faded as he turned toward Seth, and the two men seemed to notice each other for the first time.

My heart felt like it was being torn into pieces, and I looked from Victor to Seth and back again. Choosing between them would be impossible, and I shook my head, unable to even consider letting either of them go.

Seth was home. He was stability and comfort. Security and steadfastness. He was gentle and kind, teasing and charming, and seeing him in my kitchen made the big empty spot in my chest feel whole again.

Victor was passion. He was excitement and forbidden pleasure. Being with him meant throwing caution to the wind and acting on impulse. He was fiery and exciting, mysterious and unknown, and I couldn't get enough. Even as I'd walked down the hallway toward the kitchen moments earlier, my entire body had quivered with desire in anticipation of his mouth on mine and his hands on my skin, which was still sensitive from the ecstasy his touch had rendered the night before.

But as I looked back at Seth, it was though memories that had been veiled were revealed. We'd shared passion, too. We'd had that fiery, uncontrollable desire. Once upon a time, we'd been unable to keep our hands from each other, exploring and learning the meaning of pleasure together unabashed and curious, eager and unbridled, yet tender and loving. How could I have forgotten the chemistry between Seth and me?

Maybe it wasn't the explosive, lightning-hot heat I shared with Victor, but it was no less powerful.

Seth, I trusted. Seth, I knew. Seth knew me too, in ways Victor never would.

Suddenly, the old flame that had been hiding inside my chest roared from a flicker to a full-blown fire, and as though he sensed the scale sliding toward Seth, Victor's expression changed.

His eyes hardened, and his lips curled into a snarl. He squared his shoulders and lifted his chin, and from deep within me, a trembling began. Not from desire this time, but from fear.

Seth immediately stepped forward, moving me behind him.

The sunny picture in my mind began to glitch, and the tone of the dream shifted as it morphed into something different altogether.

Instead of my kitchen, the three of us stood in a room with no doors and no windows. Seth still shielded me, but Victor held a gun instead of a spatula, and he wore a dark suit in place of my whimsical apron.

I shuddered at the menacing glint in Victor's eyes as he smiled.

"Danielle, come with me."

"No," Seth growled.

I clung to Seth's arm as he stepped forward, and I screamed as Victor raised the gun and pulled the trigger.

The blast woke me, and I jerked up to sitting and scrambled backwards, still screaming as I toppled off the bed and then struggled to get to my feet.

The giant burst through the door within seconds, his gun drawn and his eyes searching the room for the source of my distress.

"Are you all right? You yelled."

"Yeah." I looked around the room in confusion, my mind dazed as I tried to decipher what was real and what was not. "I must have fallen asleep. I guess I was dreaming."

"Okay." He slid his gun back into its holster. "That's a relief. I thought someone got past us somehow. The boss just arrived. He's taking care of a small matter, but I'm sure he'll be up shortly."

He backed out and closed the door, and I did another frantic search of the room, this time looking for anything I could use as a weapon. I picked up the crystal ice bucket, and though it was heavy and could do some damage, it was also unwieldy. I wrapped my hand around the neck of the whiskey bottle instead, holding it behind my leg in hopes of the advantage of surprise.

In desperation, I moved behind the small table, my back against the wall in my attempt to get as far from the door as possible as I waited for my fate to unfold.

My eyes remained glued to the door, and it wasn't until it opened that I realized I was holding my breath.

FOURTEEN

A loud gasp escaped my lips as Victor entered the room, his eyes filled with concern as he crossed the floor to where I stood, stunned and immobile.

"God, Danielle, I've just heard what happened to you. Are you all right?" He immediately grabbed my arms to look at the bandages on my wrists, taking the whiskey bottle from me to set it back on the table. Then, he cupped my chin in his hand as he turned my head slightly left and right, examining my face. "How badly did they hurt you? You must have been terrified. George said you'd had a bad dream just now, and it's no surprise after what you've been through."

My mind moved slowly, still hazy with sleep and crippled by exhaustion and too much shock for one evening.

"What are you doing here?" I asked, uncertain if he was my hero or my villain in that moment.

He moved to wrap his arms around me, and at first, I let him, desperate for comfort and security, but then I remembered who was offering it, and I pulled out of his reach to repeat my question.

"What are you doing here?"

"What do you mean?" He squinted and cocked his head to the

side as if he were confused. "I'm here to meet you, like we planned."

The pieces began to fall into place.

"*You*? They meant *you*?" My mouth dropped open, and my eyes widened. "What the hell? You're *the boss* here? I was already on my way to you, and you had me kidnapped?"

"I did nothing of the sort. I sent you in the care of Ned and Franco to be brought here safely. You left their care, did you not?"

"Yes, but then I was taken by men who brought me here. To you! Why did you have me kidnapped?"

"I think kidnapped is a strong term."

"I was grabbed and forcefully carried against my will, placed in a chokehold, shoved in a vehicle with my hands tied behind my back, and then brought to this house without my having any choice. I'd say kidnapped is pretty damned accurate."

He clasped his hands behind his back, drawing in a slow breath. "That never should have happened. But you left the vehicle I placed you in, did you not? You insisted that Ned not follow you inside, even though he was there to ensure your safety. Ned saw Emmett's car parked on the side, so he called Emmett inside the store and asked him to keep an eye on you. Now, I do not condone Emmett's use of force or restraint, and I can assure you he's been reprimanded for it. He seemed to think you were attempting to call law enforcement, and to protect me and my interests, he made impulsive decisions."

"He kidnapped me to bring me to you. He did this for you." I needed to state it again to let my mind wrap around it.

"The way in which he performed was certainly not at my instruction. I am positive if you were to ask him now, he would tell you it was a mistake, and he's quite remorseful."

The ramifications of that statement hit me, and I stumbled a few steps farther away from him.

"Oh, so, what does that mean? Did you have him beat up? Did you break his kneecaps or smash his hand with a hammer or something?"

I braced for his answer, needing to know but not wanting to

know.

Victor's lips formed a tight, thin line, and his eyes lost their tenderness. "I'd rather not discuss the particulars. I will not tolerate anyone treating you with disrespect or laying a hand on you. That is a punishable offense, and he understands that now. Had he been a part of my team, he would have already known that, but Emmett doesn't work for me. He works for the owners of this house, Carmine and Letitia, who were dear friends of my late mother. Why were you trying to call the police?"

My thoughts had begun to clear, and as anger replaced fear and confusion, I stood straighter and crossed my arms.

"Tell me something. This man—this Emmett—he said he's been watching me for months. Was that for them...or *for you?*"

With one eyebrow cocked, Victor tilted his head and watched me, perhaps perceiving the shift in my tone.

"I needed to know you were safe." He rubbed his fingers across his chin, smoothing his goatee. "I couldn't be sure who had betrayed me from within my own team, so I reached out for help from a different angle. Given their loyalty to my mother and their proximity to your location in Cedar Creek, this family seemed the ideal answer for your protection."

"My protection? You had a total stranger you didn't even know come into my house without my knowledge. He followed me. He watched me. He toyed with me. This is your idea of protecting me?"

He frowned, and his eyes narrowed as the muscle in his jaw flexed. "Emmett was out of line. I can assure you that was never my intention. You've been under surveilled protection since the day we met, something you might not have known since your guards were instructed to handle that task with no obtrusion or interference into your daily life. However, after my arrest and your move to Florida, my options became limited, and as I mentioned before, I had to rely on others to manage personnel decisions. The guard originally assigned to you in Cedar Creek accompanied Carmine and Letitia when they left recently for an extensive trip in Europe. Emmett was assigned as a replacement, and I regret to learn that he may not have been a wise choice."

"The guy is a psychopath! He stole my nightgown, for Christ's sake, and God only knows what else he may have done in my house. I'm surprised I wasn't assaulted." I looked down and held up my hands, putting my bandaged wrists in front of his face. "Oh, wait. What am I saying? I was assaulted!"

Victor's eyes darkened, and he spoke through a clenched jaw. "And for that, he has paid a price. But given what you're telling me now, perhaps the retribution he's received isn't enough."

His tone sent shivers down my spine, and I was reminded how surreal my life had become. Whereas in the past, the two of us might have been discussing whether DiCaprio's character was still dreaming at the end of *Inception* or which of the Beatles was the most talented, I suspected that now if I didn't take care with my words, I might be sentencing a man to his death for stepping across a line that was already beyond normal boundaries.

I stared at Victor, searching his face for the familiar. Had he always looked this menacing? Had his voice always held such a calculating edge? Perhaps I'd been blind to it all and I'd glossed over what I didn't want to see. Were my memories even accurate?

The man I'd thought I loved spoke of unity, compassion, environmental conservation, and an appreciation of the arts. The man who stood before me looked much like him but spoke so casually of punishment, surveillance, and retribution that it seemed impossible the two were the same.

"So much for the changed man, eh?" I said, my voice quiet in the deafening stillness of the room. "Are we not even going to pretend anymore? You're just fully embracing your true identity now and hoping I'll do the same?"

His anger seemed to dissipate, and his expression softened into something akin to apologetic.

"Danielle, please—"

"Tell me the truth for once. There never was a deal with the feds, was there? They didn't pardon you and ten of your closest men and buy you all a one-way ticket out of the country. That was all a lie."

He rubbed his hand across his face and gazed toward the ceiling. Then he lifted the lid off the crystal ice bucket and dropped a couple of cubes into each of the two glasses that sat on the table. After pouring whiskey in them both, he offered me one, shrugging when I refused. Then he sat in the chair by the window, and after a long sip of his drink, he lay his head back against the chair and stared at me through half-closed eyes.

I'd never seen him look so exhausted—his shoulders drooping, his mouth drawn, and his eyes uncharacteristically dull.

"I never lied to you in that regard," he said, his voice thick, slow, and tired. "I promise you that a deal was made. Federal officers were involved and agreed to the terms." He took another sip of whiskey and waved the glass toward me. "Now, it might not fit the profile of the traditional witness protection that you think you're familiar with, and it certainly won't be publicly recorded with the courts, but I didn't lie. I was released from federal custody and given passage out of the country. I was also given leeway to choose my traveling companions."

"So, a crooked deal. A back door deal." I nodded with understanding, surprised by the inexplicable disappointment I felt. Why should it matter to me whether or not he was telling the truth or whether his deal was legitimate? It wasn't like we could ever go back after all that had been revealed. Hell, it wasn't like we had anything of substance to go back to.

But still, I suppose a tiny part of me had hoped he wasn't lying. I'd hoped that he was redeemable, and that fact would in some way redeem me and the choices I'd made. "What about you turning? You said you gave evidence on powerful people, and they were pissed about it. Was that all creative truth as well?"

He shrugged again. "I gave them things. I gave them people. I gave them enough to get what I wanted without putting too much of a target on my head. Or yours."

"And yet, you led me to believe my life was in imminent danger. You said on the phone tonight that my house was being watched. That there were people in Cedar Creek bent on doing me harm. But the man I thought was following me was your guy, or there on your behalf anyway. Was there ever anyone else? Or was that all a lie to get me to come to you?"

He drained the whiskey glass and set it on the table, and then with a loud sigh, he cracked his knuckles, which he knew I hated. "The world doesn't work the way you'd like to believe, my love. You don't always see the people watching you, and you don't always know who is a threat and who means you harm. I didn't lie, but let me ask you a question. If I had simply called and told you I'd been released and was about to leave the country, would you have come to me?"

"No. Definitely not."

He frowned and twisted his lips together with a slight nod.

"I suppose I expected that. And yet, I am certain we are destined to be together." A faint smile played at his lips, and the tenderness returned to his eyes. "So certain that I was willing to delay my own escape and jeopardize my own freedom and that of my men to come for you, and I'm delaying it still. We should have already been in the air. We've wasted crucial time finding you, and now we waste more time ensuring that the officers you've involved aren't on our trail. Every minute we delay increases our risk."

"Am I supposed to feel bad about that? I never asked you to make that sacrifice, and given the choice—which I was not—I would have told you not to waste your time."

Leaning forward to brace his elbows on his knees, he smiled broadly, and a flicker of memory flitted through my mind. Another time, another place, that same grin, and much different emotions attached to it.

"Do you remember the first day we met?" he asked. "We talked the evening away through the night and into the early hours of the morning. I'd never in my life conversed with someone that much for that long. God, it was like I wanted the clock to stop. I didn't want the sun to rise and bring the day. I never imagined I would find another soul I felt so connected to. Whatever topic arose—from melting ice caps to philosophy to the government's errant strides in foreign policy to the best way to eat an ice cream cone—we were in step and in sync."

Despite my resolve and the barricade I'd built inside me, a pang of longing and loss gripped my heart.

I did remember that day, that night. How could I not? It was as though I'd been struck by lightning the first moment I laid eyes on him, and that current had continued surging through me the more we talked during that first encounter, the spark growing so powerful it was all I could do to maintain control. We'd stayed up until four in the morning, and I'd counted down the hours at work the next day until I could see him again. He'd been waiting at my front door when I arrived home that next evening, and we tore at each other's clothes and explored a physical connection even more explosive than our mental one. My fate had been sealed in that joining, and despite only knowing each other twenty-four hours at that point, we both knew we couldn't be apart. He stayed that night and never left.

Well, until they dragged him away in handcuffs.

I sat on the foot of the bed and gripped the post, trying to hold onto reality and not be sucked into the memories of something that was never as it seemed. I'd mourned the loss of that man. I'd grieved his absence as though he'd died, because in so many ways, he had. Except here he was, coming to kneel on one knee in front of me—all at once the same man, and yet not the same at all.

Victor took my hands in his and looked up at me, his eyes pleading once more. "I knew when I awoke that first morning with you in my arms that my life had been changed. I knew then that I would do whatever it took to be worthy of you and to spend my life with you. I went to my uncle that day and told him I wanted out. I told him I would agree to whatever conditions he required if he would allow me to go and pursue a life of my own."

"What did he say?" I asked, even though the answer was obvious.

"He refused, of course," Victor said with a grimace, "but I was undeterred. You had awakened something in me that couldn't be ignored. I began to divest myself of any interests in the family business. I began to sever ties, and as you can imagine now knowing what you do, my actions were met with swift retribution, first in the form of lectures, then in the form of action."

So, while I'd gone to work each day and struggled to stay focused on the administrative tasks at hand, Victor had been attempting to resign from his life as a killer for a crime syndicate. It still seemed too surreal to comprehend.

Part of me wanted to turn from him and not hear any more. After all, what good would it do? What would it matter? But another part of me—the journalist in me, perhaps—held way too much curiosity to keep him from telling me what I'd longed to know. For the past two years, I'd had so many unanswered questions. So much time spent reexamining every word, every action, every memory.

"What happened?" I asked. "Did *they* have you arrested? Your family? That makes no sense! Wouldn't you be a greater threat to them if you were in jail and could provide evidence?"

"It was never their intention for me to go to jail." He looked down at our intertwined hands. "Orders had been given, and my life had been timestamped, but Valentina, who is more a sister to me than a cousin, could not bear to see me killed, so when she discovered what was planned, she tried to thwart them. She trusted the wrong person and ended up turning me over to the feds instead."

I'd always wondered why he was arrested, what it was that had been the turning point to get him caught. I'd pondered afterward, once the situation became clear, if perhaps his involvement with me and our rushed marriage might have compromised him in some way. Again, now, as I had then, I marveled at all that must have gone on behind the scenes while I went about my days and nights oblivious to what he was dealing with. How could I not have known something was amiss? How could there have been no outward signs?

Easily, I suppose, when I considered that I didn't know Victor that well at all. I wouldn't have recognized his tells like I would have with Seth. I wouldn't have noticed the slight changes in mood if he was apprehensive or the difference in his voice if he was scared. We'd had no time to record all those things, to experience them together and catalog them for easy reference. I was so caught up in the whirlwind of romance, passion, and promises that I didn't delve deep enough. I didn't take the time to get to know the man I had pledged my life to.

"I had no idea," I said, my voice barely above a whisper, the statement meant for me more than for him.

"I didn't want you to know," he said, cupping my cheek in his hand. "I wanted to protect you from that world, from that part of my life. It was wrong of me not to tell you the truth. It was wrong of me to think we could live in a bubble where the past didn't exist, and the present and the future could be of my own choosing. I'm sorry for that, for what I put you through. But now, here we are, sweetness. Everything is out in the open. No more secrets. We have the opportunity to start over. To start fresh." He moved closer, his eyes on my lips. "I know we shared a connection most people never experience. I know you felt it every bit as much as I did. Let's not turn our backs on that." His mouth was so close I could feel his breath when he spoke. "Let's not walk away from the purest emotion we've ever felt."

I shook my head and pulled away. "It wasn't pure. It was based on lies. How would I ever trust anything you tell me after this?"

"Because I'm telling you that I will be honest with you. If you're willing to give me another chance—to give *us* another chance—no topic will be off-limits. Moving forward, I'm an open book. No shadow life, no secrets. If there's anything you want to know, any question you need answered, I'm willing. I'm yours. I believe we can work through this. I believe our love is strong enough to withstand this, and that we can come out even stronger on the other side."

He moved again to kiss me, and I turned my head.

"It's not love if you're forcing me to come with you."

Drawing back, his eyes wide with surprise, he frowned. "I'm not.

You agreed to come. You said you would listen. That you would give me a chance."

"I said that because I didn't want you to kill Seth."

His frown deepened. "You think so little of me as to assume I would do that? You think I could ever kill him knowing what he meant to you?"

"It shouldn't matter whether he means anything to me or not. You shouldn't kill anyone!" I stood and moved past him to pace the room. "I could never get past that, Victor. I could never accept the fact that you've killed people. That you've taken lives."

"Never of the innocent."

"And that makes it right?" I stopped and flung my hands outward. "It makes it okay to kill if they deserved to die in your mind?"

Standing, he moved toward me, but then paused as though he didn't want to crowd me.

"It's not okay, and I know that." He ran his hands through his hair. "It was a way of life I'd been brought up in, but it's not who I am or who I want to be. That's done now, I assure you. I won't ever be involved in anything like that again. I give you my word."

"And yet, you're surrounded by your henchmen. Men who think nothing of beating the shit out of strangers without asking any questions first or grabbing women from convenience stores and placing them in chokeholds. How is your life now any different?"

He placed his hands on his hips and raised his chin. "Until we get out of the country, we are not safe. I will do what I must to protect you, and I will not apologize for that."

"But what if it is *you* I most need protection from?"

His brows came together with his frown, and the confusion in his eyes seemed tinged with pain.

"I would never hurt you," he whispered.

"You already have." The dull ache of pain that had resided in my chest since the morning of his arrest sharpened and clamped down on my heart, taking my breath. I'd done all I could to numb it for the past two years, but it could no longer be ignored. It festered and burned inside me, raw and exposed. "You nearly destroyed me. It was worse than if you had died, and it has taken every ounce of strength I have to put you behind me and try to move forward with my life. Now, you show up and you expect me to somehow, to just—"

My voice fell away, and he rushed forward to put his arms around me, and though my mind screamed for me to push him away, the wound in the deepest recesses of my heart was desperate to be soothed, even if only for a moment.

"I will make it up to you," he said, his voice breaking with emotion as he pressed his forehead to mine. "There's nothing I wouldn't do for you. No lengths I wouldn't go to for you. You are my life and my heart."

"Let me go." My voice trembled, barely audible as I struggled to push the words out. "If you truly love me, if you truly care for me, then let me go. Let me continue rebuilding my life without you in it. Without being watched or followed or coerced. If you love me, set me free."

His arms tightened around me, and his eyes darted back and forth as he searched mine. "Give me a chance first. Fly away with me. Give me...two months. That's the amount of time we had before, and it changed my life forever. Give me two months and I'll prove I'm worthy of your love. I will prove we can be happy together."

"You can't fix this, Victor. Our happiness was based on lies, and I don't feel the same knowing the truth. The man I loved does not exist. He never existed. He was some weird meshed creation of our combined imaginations."

"No. No, no, no. I am who I was with you. I'm here. It's me. We'll go away, far away from anything that happened here. I know a place, a perfect place for the honeymoon we should have had. We'll sleep in an open-air bungalow over the Indian Ocean. We'll eat fresh-caught fish daily and have decadent desserts made with coconut and pineapples. We'll sip on tropical drinks—well, I'll have whiskey brought in for you—and we'll watch the sun set and debate the merits of British humor and learn to make our own fried yams. We'll take the time to really get to know one another. Nothing hidden. Just you and me and the wind and the waves."

I removed myself from his grasp and stepped away from the future he described.

"I don't want to leave with you. I want to go home, and I want your assurance that I won't be watched or followed or killed in my sleep. That I won't have to worry about my family or my business. I want my life to be my own again, as though we'd never met."

He straightened and placed his hands on his hips. "You love me. I know you do. If we could just get away from here—"

I shook my head and looked him in the eye as I spoke my truth. "No. I loved your idealized version of yourself, but after seeing who you really are, there's no way I could feel the same way about you. I'm repulsed by you, and nothing will change that."

He took a step back, almost a stumble, really, as though I'd shoved him. His eyes widened, and then they narrowed, his nostrils flaring and his gaze hardening as it shifted past me. He left the room without another word.

What had I done? Had I gone too far? What had I set in motion with my callous words? I'd spoken with honesty from my heart, but perhaps in light of who I was dealing with, I should have filtered my message and used more caution.

He'd seemed so calm and rational as we talked that I'd somehow neglected to remember I was dealing with a ruthless killer whose moral code dictated that he play by a different set of rules.

Would he be capable of just letting me walk away? Was there enough of the Victor I'd known inside him to grant me my freedom? Or had I just signed my own death warrant?

I went straight to the glass of whiskey he'd poured for me and downed it in two gulps, and then I poured another glass and sat on the edge of the chair as my knees threatened to buckle and my body began to tremble uncontrollably.

FIFTEEN

oon after Victor left the room, a knock at the door startled me.

"Yes?" I called out, standing to face the unknown.

The giant opened the door and came in to hand me my purse.

"Thank you!" I grabbed it from him and immediately looked inside, eager to find my phone and contact Seth. "Do you know—"

He had already left and closed the door before I could ask if I'd be leaving soon.

Surely, that was what this meant, right? Why would Victor return my purse if he hadn't intended to let me go?

Not seeing my cell phone, I dumped the contents onto the bed, raking my hand through my things. It was no use. The phone wasn't there. Had it been left behind at the motel? I struggled to remember where it was when all the chaos erupted. I'd been holding it, using it for a stopwatch, when Seth returned. I squeezed my eyes shut and tried to remember what I'd done with it. Everything had happened so quickly once I saw him through the peephole, but I thought I remembered laying it on the chair when I reached to unlock the door.

Damn!

I wanted to call Seth. I wanted to know that he was okay. I wanted him to know I was okay, for now, at least.

The memory of being in his arms earlier came back to me, and I swallowed at the lump in my throat, pushing down the emotions that threatened to overtake me. Why had I been such an idiot to let him go? Why had I been so damned stubborn, so determined to leave him behind?

I never really had, of course. He'd always been there. In my mind. In my heart. Even as I moved on with my life and encountered new experiences, I'd still imagine telling him about them. Wondering what he would think or how he would react. At some point, it had become too painful, and I'd barricaded my mind against his memory, but he'd never left my heart.

It was odd to consider that within the span of a few hours, I'd been in the company of the only two men I'd ever loved. Despite the commonalities in their appearance, they couldn't be more different in every other way imaginable, nor could our relationships and the way they had developed. As I considered my feelings for both men, I reached some difficult conclusions.

I'd been infatuated with Victor, driven more by lust than love. I'd thought at the time it was more, but after seeing him tonight, I was able to look back with more clarity. I could acknowledge I'd been swept up in the idea of love at first sight and a whirlwind romance that flew in the face of what everyone expected from me. A lonely life and a long dry spell without physical affection had made me suscep-tible to falling fast and hard. The truth was I hadn't really known Victor at all, certainly not enough to determine if I genuinely loved him.

Seeing Seth again, on the other hand, reminded me what a deep connection we'd shared. Despite the years that had passed since we'd been together, everything I'd felt for him had been right there beneath the surface, and if anything, the surreal events of the night had made it more clear to me than ever how much I'd missed him in my life.

I resolved that if Victor allowed me to go and I escaped my Mafia entanglement with my life intact, I'd do everything in my power to right the wrongs I'd done to Seth. If I could only be granted the chance to see him again, to hold him again, I'd never be stupid enough to let him go.

With that decision made, my determination to leave solidified. I wouldn't sit cowering in my lush prison cell, waiting for word from Victor as to my fate. I'd simply demand to leave. Surely, he wouldn't kill me after going to all this trouble to be with me. If he felt for me the way he said he did, he'd have to let me go. To let me live. Wouldn't he?

As I grabbed my things to put them back in the purse, I noticed a passport. I opened it, shocked to see my name and a photo of me above a signature so close to mine that I did a double-take.

I'd never had a passport. I'd never needed one.

Wow. Victor had been quite prepared in planning our escape. He'd obviously known before tonight that he'd be released if he'd had a forgery of this quality created.

What else had been put in place for our new lives? Where else had my signature been forged without my knowledge?

It didn't matter, because I wasn't leaving with Victor.

I shoved the fake passport into my purse and slung the strap over my shoulder before going to the door and flinging it open, ready to demand my release.

The giant raised an eyebrow as I descended the staircase and strode toward him with purpose.

"I'd like to leave now," I said, forcing confidence into my voice. "Can you direct me to a phone so I can call a cab?"

He chuckled and reached up to scratch the side of his head. "I believe transportation has already been arranged. If you'd like to wait in your room, it shouldn't be too much longer now."

"Oh, thank you." I went back upstairs to the bedroom, closing the door behind me and then leaning against it in relief as I allowed the tension to ebb from my body.

Victor was going to let me go. My honesty had gotten through to him, and whatever feelings he had for me and whatever decency existed in him had prevailed. Or perhaps the delays I'd caused had finally become too great a cost and he'd decided it was best to go without me. I didn't really care what had changed his mind. I only cared that I was about to be free.

Where would his men take me? I couldn't imagine they'd drive me all the way back home. It was more than an hour, and they had a plane to catch. Of course, just because Victor was leaving didn't mean all his associates were traveling with him. Undoubtedly, there would be some left behind.

More than likely, they'd take me back to the motel where they'd picked me up. There was no way Seth would still be there. Once Tristan had arrived, I had no doubt Seth would have refused any medical treatment and insisted on joining Tristan in the search for me and the effort to catch Victor. I wished I had some way to let Seth know I was fine. I hated to think of how worried he must be.

Of course, no matter how relieved he'd be to find out I was free and clear, he'd also be disappointed if Victor got away. And for all I knew, Victor might already be on his way to the plane, choosing to be safely in the air and away from the chance of capture before releasing me. He'd been aware I had tried to contact law enforcement at the convenience store, so it would have been understandable on his part if he'd wanted a head start before letting me loose with information on his whereabouts.

I was surprisingly okay with that. I'd already said everything I needed to say to Victor. We had no unfinished business between us. And as far as him being caught and serving his time, while I had no doubt he deserved it, I was selfishly fine with him leaving the country. In an odd way, it felt comforting to know he wouldn't be on the same continent with me. I wouldn't have to fear what might happen if he broke out of jail again, and if he found happiness on the island paradise he'd described, he'd be less likely to come back or to harbor resentments toward me.

As my fears subsided and hope began to flourish inside me, the adrenaline I'd been thriving on dwindled, leaving me exhausted and spent. Yawning, I tossed my purse on the bed and then moved to the sink to splash water on my face. I couldn't afford to let my guard down just yet. I needed to stay alert a little while longer.

I had just pressed the soft towel to my face when Bea knocked and then entered.

"Here we are," she said, her voice upbeat with a singsong quality. She rolled a suitcase in with her and lifted it to the bed before opening it.

"What's this?" I asked.

Ignoring my question, she pulled out a burgundy silk dress and shook it out before grabbing a hanger from the closet for it.

"Oh, good. It's not too wrinkled. I was worried we'd need to steam it. I suppose that bodes well for travel."

I shook my head to try and clear it so I could think. "What are you talking about?"

"Don't worry. You'll be able to change into something more comfortable once you're in the air, but I was instructed that you'd need to wear this for the initial leg of your journey."

"No, you don't understand." I held my hands up in protest of her assertions. "The plans have changed, and I won't be traveling with Victor. Someone is supposed to be taking me home."

Bea raised an eyebrow and clasped her hands together.

"I'm simply doing what I was asked to do. If there are any changes, you'll need to take that up with someone much higher up the ladder than me, I'm afraid." She turned in dismissal and pulled a pink cosmetic bag from the suitcase. "Now, I'm told your desired toiletry brands are in here for your shower, facial care, and make-up. If there's anything else you need, please let me know. Given the hour, I might be limited in what I can procure, but I'll try."

"No, I don't need any toiletries or clothes, and I won't be showering. If you'll just speak to Victor, I'm sure he will tell you that I'm no longer accompanying him."

She nodded and moved toward the door. "Very well, then. I'll leave that between the two of you.

I waited only a moment before flinging the door open to follow her, unwilling to be left out of the discussion with Victor regarding my future.

The two of them stood in the dark at the end of the hallway, Bea's murmured account of our conversation whispered too softly for me to make out any details.

Victor looked up and made eye contact with me as he patted Bea's shoulder. "I'll take care of it. Thank you."

Walking toward me slowly with his hands in his pockets and his gaze on the carpet, he only looked up again once he'd come to a stop in front of me. He motioned for me to step inside the bedroom, but I ignored the request and stood firm in the hallway.

With a deep inhale and a long, slow exhale, he leaned his shoulder against the wall and crossed his arms, his exhaustion even more apparent than it had been before. The light from the bedroom fell across his face, which looked paler than I'd ever seen it. His mouth was drawn tight in a hard, grim line, and his eyelids seemed so heavy that it looked as though he might fall asleep standing up.

"I'm ready to go home now," I said, my voice more timid than I'd intended. I crossed my arms to mimic his, lifting my chin and hoping I looked less scared than I felt.

Rubbing his hand roughly over his chin, he lifted his tired eyes to meet mine. I shivered at the steely determination I saw there.

"I can't let you do that."

He spoke quietly, but the force of his words knocked me a step backwards.

"Victor, I want to go home." My voice was hoarse with fear.

"Sweetness, this might seem unpleasant now, but it will all be worth it in the end. I've told you there's nothing I wouldn't do for you, no lengths I wouldn't go to, and if this is what it takes, then I'm willing to bear the brunt of your wrath now to keep our future intact."

"No," I said, shaking my head as his intentions became clear. "No! I won't go. I won't leave with you."

He straightened, and the telltale muscle in his jaw pulsed as he spoke. "We're meant to be together. You are my destiny, and I am yours. We will work through our issues as husband and wife. Hell, I'll even agree to counseling, if that's what you want. But there's no way for our relationship to survive with you here and me across the world from you. We must be together for this to work."

"It's not going to work! I don't love you. I don't want to be with you."

"You *do* love me, and eventually, you'll remember that. I'll make you remember how happy we were. You'll see."

The relief I'd felt before dissipated, and my mind reeled with the renewed direness of my situation. "It will be outright kidnapping if you make me get on that plane. I will fight you every step of the way."

His shrug, though casual, seemed menacing, as though he'd already reached that conclusion and was fine with it.

"If that's what it takes to have you by my side," he confirmed. With a cold stare that gave me chills, he took a step toward me. "Look, you're angry with me, I know. If I had more time, I'd give you the space you need. I'd court you. I'd take things slowly, proving to you that we can be who we were together. But circumstances dictate that I have to leave the country, and I have to go now. I've already delayed my departure far past what was prudent in my efforts to get you to agree to come with me."

"What did it matter if I agreed when you plan to take me no matter what?" Even as I said it, I shuddered at his conviction and my fate.

He moved closer, and I tried to retreat, but my back hit the wall. He braced his hands against the wood paneling on either side of my head and leaned forward, his face inches from mine.

"I don't want to take you against your will. I want you to desire our future together. I want you to remember what we had and to believe we can still have it. It would be my wish that you would come not only willingly, but eagerly."

"That's not going to happen."

He reached to trace my bottom lip with his thumb. "I see now that it was too rushed. Too sudden. You haven't had time to think things through. You haven't had time to work through your anger and see past it. I knew you'd be resistant to picking up and leaving without any warning, but I'd foolishly hoped that when we saw each other, your love for me would be enough to get us on the plane and on our way."

"Yeah, well, I guess you underestimated how much I loathe you right now."

"Obviously," he said, his mouth turning up on one side into an uneven grin. "And so, we move to Plan B, my love."

It took everything in me not to lunge at him, to claw at his eyes and spit in his face.

"Is this the one where you just take me and hold me prisoner and prove you're every bit the monster they described in that courtroom?"

His lips twisted and the muscle in his jaw began to flex again. "It is not my intent to hold you prisoner. You have my word that you'll be treated with the respect you deserve as my wife."

"I'm not your wife," I spat out.

He arched an eyebrow and flicked his head to the side as if the statement were debatable.

"If you won't come on the plane willingly, I'll have you carried on," he said, standing up straight as he shoved his hands back in his pockets. "But I will not let you go, and since I can't return to this country once I leave it, I must take you with me and make things up to you once we're safe."

I pulled myself from the wall and shifted so that the stairs were behind me as I stepped away from him.

"Safe? How would I ever feel safe with you, Victor? If you would do this to me, how on earth would I *ever* feel safe? What else would you do to me once you force me on a plane and carry me to some godforsaken island?"

"I would never hurt you, sweetness."

"You keep saying that, but you've already proven that's a lie, like everything else."

A flicker of anger flashed in his eyes, and he closed the short distance between us and grabbed my face in his hands, his gaze intent on my lips.

Shoving against his chest, I turned to run for the stairs.

I hadn't heard Ned approach behind me, and crashing into him was like hitting a brick wall as he stepped forward to block my escape. His arms wrapped around me as he lifted me off the ground, and despite the pain from my still sore ribs, I began to kick and scream with every bit of adrenaline and strength I could muster. Ned held me tighter, grinning as though he enjoyed my predicament, and my stomach turned in on itself with a wave of nausea as the air was cut off from my lungs.

"Release her," Victor growled behind me.

Ned's grin faded. "I don't think it's a good idea, boss." His arms closed even tighter around me. "She'll just run again."

"I said release my wife, now."

Ned let go immediately, and I tumbled to the ground.

Victor came to my side to help me up, and I jerked my arm from his grasp. "Don't touch me."

I stood, crowded between Victor and Ned in the narrow hallway as I pressed my hands to my tender ribs and took in a ragged breath.

"Leave us," Victor said to Ned, and then he pulled me into the bedroom and shut the door. "You can spew your anger all you want, and I'll take it because I deserve it, but you *will* leave with me, one way or another. We made vows. We pledged our lives until death do us part, and if there's one thing you should know about my family, it's that we never break a vow."

"Your lies made those vows null and void, and the state of Illinois granted me a divorce that freed me from them."

"We were joined together in the eyes of God."

I laughed in disbelief. "Really? You're going to bring God into this? Because I'm pretty sure murder is high on His list of things to avoid."

"Enough!" Anger glittered brightly in his eyes, which were fully open and alert now. He grabbed my arms, his fingers digging into my flesh as he stood towering over me. "No more delays. I'm done pleading and reasoning. I didn't want to have to do this, but you leave me no choice."

SIXTEEN

Fear gripped me, and I fought to hang onto my fury. "Do what? Tie me up? Carry me onto the plane kicking and screaming? Because that's what you'll have to do to make me go with you, and I'll hate you for it. And don't think for a minute that my family won't come after you. They'll never stand for this."

"Texts will be sent to your family from your phone as soon as we're in the air. They'll be told you've decided to give our marriage another chance, and that you'll be traveling but will contact them whenever we arrive."

I shook my head. "They'll know it's a lie. They've seen what you did to me. They'll know I would never leave with you."

His dark grin was cold and calculating, and gooseflesh rippled across my skin in response.

"Love makes people do crazy things, sweetness. They never would have thought you would get married after knowing someone only two weeks, and yet, you did just that without even telling them first. Why would they question what you would do for me now?"

Guilt washed over me for the way I'd treated my family, and some part of me suspected he was right. They no longer trusted me.

They no longer trusted my judgment. They probably would believe I'd left with him.

"Seth would know," I said, clinging to a sudden hope.

His grin widened, and another wave of nausea hit me. "Would he now? You yourself told him you were willing to leave with me."

"No. Seth knows me. He knew I was bluffing for him. He knows there's no way I would actually go. He'll come for me. He won't stop searching until he finds me. Until he finds you! He'll make you pay for this."

Victor chuckled and rolled his eyes. "Really? He didn't even follow you to Chicago when you were his, and you think he's going to bother to leave the country for you now when you're not? The last time he saw you, you were in my arms. You had your tongue down my throat and your breasts shoved against me, and I looked him in the eye as I cupped your beautiful ass in my hands and asserted my claim on you. He watched you walk out the door with me willingly."

I shook my head, reviled at the memory of what I'd had to do in the motel room. "He knows I did that for him. He knows I did what it took for him to be safe. I played a part to get you away from him."

"And you don't think he has any doubts? You don't think he wonders if perhaps you wanted to come with me?"

My facade faltered as his dart hit its target. Seth might doubt. He'd questioned why I approached him in the bar. He'd questioned several times during our circular escape whether I intended to meet up with Victor, whether I'd resisted him accompanying me due to my desire to be reunited with Victor. If I didn't return, he might think I'd decided to go away with Victor, to reconcile and forgive.

But, no. Seth knew me better than I knew myself. He would know there was no way I'd leave my family like that. Especially not with Amy ready to give birth so soon. Seth would know I wouldn't be willing to miss that.

Would he also know how much he meant to me? How good it had felt to reconnect with him over the course of the evening? Would he have any idea how much I wanted another chance with him? Had it felt as right to him as it did to me?

He'd told me on the dance floor he'd never gotten over me, that I was the reason his relationships since us hadn't worked out. But he hadn't said he loved me, and we hadn't discussed the future at all. His focus had been getting me through the evening alive.

So, after all that had transpired, after all I'd done to him, would he still want me? Would he still fight for me? Would he come after me?

Or was Victor right? Would Seth simply assume I'd embraced insanity and run away with a killer?

"Ah, I see that you know I'm right." Victor smiled at my discomfort.

"No," I shook my head, refusing to accept that possibility. "You're wrong. Seth knows me. He knows I wouldn't go with you. He will find me, and he'll make you pay for the hell you've put me through."

Victor's wicked smile faded, and his jaw tightened as the anger returned to his eyes once again.

"You're still so hung up on him, aren't you? Well, I might as well make that work in my favor. I won't have to carry you on that plane, and you won't fight me at all." His voice was cold and his gaze even colder. "I can make you get on that plane easily, and yes, you may hate me for it, but I'm willing to risk that to have you by my side."

He pulled his phone from his pocket and swiped his fingers across the screen before flipping it around to show me a picture.

Seth sat slumped in a chair, blindfolded and gagged with his hands still secured behind him.

I gasped in shock and reached for the phone, but Victor held it beyond my grasp.

"Where is he? He's supposed to be safe. You told me you'd get him help once we left the hotel room."

"He's safe," Victor said, sliding the phone into his back pocket. "For now. And I said I'd call for help once we were clear of the area, which—thanks to you and your delays—we are not yet. But the deal still stands. You come with me, willingly and without protest, and I guarantee the deputy won't be harmed."

My legs failed me, and I sank onto the bed. Nothing remained of the Victor I'd known and thought I'd loved. The man standing before me with his hands resting casually on his hips as he stared down at me was a killer. A monster. Ruthless and determined to have what he wanted. Me.

For the first time, I saw him clearly and without any filter or veil, and my stomach convulsed in disgust. Fear rippled across my skin in gooseflesh as the magnitude of his vileness struck me.

I knew without any doubt that Seth wasn't safe, and neither was my family. The only hope I could give them, the only way I could have a chance of protecting them, was to do as Victor asked.

The weight of that truth crushed me, forcing all the air from my lungs. I opened my mouth to gulp in more, but my chest refused to expand, so I resorted to short, shallow breaths, which made me feel even more dizzy and lightheaded.

Victor showed no outward emotion as he watched me struggle to breathe, and finally, I gathered enough oxygen to force words out between my lips.

"Once we leave, how do I know you won't go back on your word and kill him anyway?"

"You don't," he said, his voice still hard. "You have to trust me."

I shook my head and closed my eyes against the tears that threatened to spill. "But I don't trust you. I can't trust you."

He bent and placed his hands on the bed on either side of me. Opening my eyes, I found his face only inches from mine. I tried to draw back, but he grabbed my chin with a firm grip.

"Then let me make the choice easier for you," he whispered. "Either you get on that plane, or I'll have my men make him wish he'd never met you."

My heart pounded so hard that the force of it thudded in my head, turning the room red with rage and terror.

"You really are a monster," I spat out between gritted teeth.

"No." He released my chin and stood to stare down at me. "I just meant what I said when I told you I'd do whatever it took to have you. I've tried everything I can to do it your way, but you haven't made it easy. So, now we'll do it my way. Take a shower and get dressed in the clothes I provided." He opened the door and stepped into the hallway. "Bea? Could you come here, please?"

A door farther down the hall opened. "Yes, sir?"

"I need my wife ready to depart in thirty minutes, so please assist her with whatever she needs." He looked back at me. "Wear the burgundy dress. It's always been my favorite color on you, and we'll be making a stop along the way to meet with an associate I'd like to impress."

Bea didn't look at me or Victor as she came into the room with her head bowed. It would have been impossible not to feel the tension, but if she noticed it, she never let on. As soon as Victor left and closed the door behind him, she pulled a roll of tape from her pocket and held it up.

"I've brought a roll of waterproof tape to wrap your bandages so they don't get ruined."

She lifted my hand in hers to expose my wrist as she pulled at the tape with her teeth, and I didn't even bother to resist. Defeat washed over me, and silent tears streamed down my cheeks as Bea tenderly wrapped my wrists and cut the tape.

When she had finished, she gave my right arm a pat and then went to turn on the water in the shower.

"I'll give you a moment's privacy for the shower, and then I'll be back in to assist you."

"I don't need any assistance." I huffed as I wiped away my tears.

"Very well." Bea nodded and walked toward the door.

Suddenly, a thought occurred to me and I couldn't let her leave the room without at least trying.

"Bea?"

She stopped and turned with a sympathetic smile beneath her blue eyes and raised eyebrows. "Yes?"

"There is one way you could assist me." I tried to recall any details I'd seen in the picture of Seth. "Can you tell me if there's a room in this house with white walls and a wide gray stripe at about chair rail height running around the room? There's a gray table in the center of the room."

Her smile faded, and her eyes grew wary.

"Please, Bea. Do you know of a room like that here? Or do you know of any other place that might have a room that looks like that? It would probably be close by. Maybe an office building or something?"

"I would suggest you get in the shower, dear. The clock is ticking."

"Please, I'm begging you. I understand that you're simply trying to do your job. I respect that. And I also understand that in your opinion, I chose this situation when I married Victor, but just so you know, I didn't know what I was marrying into. He hid all that from me. And yes, I should have taken more time to get to know him, certainly more time before marrying him, but none of that changes his dishonesty and that what he presented wasn't true. I'm willing to pay the price for my mistake, but a man's life is in danger right now because of me, and he doesn't deserve to die." My voice broke as my mind replayed the image of Seth beaten, bound, and gagged. "He tried to help me. He tried to protect me, and now, he's being punished for my sins. He's innocent in all this, Bea, and I can't bear to have him suffer for me. Please? Do you have any idea where he might be? If there's any way I could help him, or at the very least, if I could just get a message to him—to tell him I'm sorry. To tell him that I love him."

She chuckled as she shook her head. "You've sentenced this man to his death, and now you want to sentence me to mine? You haven't learned anything from your mistakes, it seems."

"I mean you no harm at all, and I pray I haven't sentenced Seth to his death. The only reason I'm agreeing to go with Victor is to save Seth. Victor promised he'll get help for Seth's injuries and that he'll let him go if I get on the plane."

"Are you really as foolish as you seem?" She cocked her head to one side as she crossed her arms. "After rejecting your husband, you rubbed it in his face that your love and loyalty is given freely to another man, and you think he'll let that man live? You know less about this family's lifestyle than you think you do." She brushed me away with her hand as she turned to go, but then she stopped at the doorway and looked over her shoulder in my direction. "You'd best get moving, my dear. His patience has its limits, even for you."

As I stepped beneath the stream of hot water, it wasn't lost on me that my desire for a shower was what had spun everything out of control. If I hadn't wanted so desperately to be clean, Seth wouldn't have left the room, and we would have been together with at least a barrier of locked doors between us and the danger that lurked outside. Tristan's men would have had more time to find Victor, and Seth would likely be uninjured and by my side still. I lay my cheek against the cool tile and tried to quell the panic inside me.

Would he release Seth as he'd promised? Would I have any way of knowing that Seth was okay? That my sacrifice had worked? Maybe I could insist on Victor providing proof. Pictures of Seth with a doctor, or even better, a call from Seth to let me know he'd been freed.

But Bea was right. Victor's patience was wearing thin. I'd denied him. I'd rejected him. I'd revealed my hand, and I had no leverage left to make demands. I was certain now that I'd be forced on the plane whether I agreed or not, and Seth's fate would be determined by Victor's jealousy and need for revenge more than any action on my part.

What about my family, though? Could I at least buy their safety if I changed my attitude? Perhaps if I tried hard enough to charm Victor and go along with his plans, I could be convincing enough to negotiate their safety. It was the only straw left to grasp.

Images flooded my mind, and I shoved my fist in my mouth to keep from screaming in rage and pain. My sister smiling as she cradled her belly, my mother and father holding their first grandchild,

Seth's eyes vulnerable and unguarded as he'd looked at me on the dance floor tonight.

How could I save them all? How could I keep my mistake from touching them?

I had to play my part through to the end. I had to make Victor happy again. Get him on my side. I had to convince him that doing these favors for me would pay off for him in the end. It was obvious that what he thought was love for me was more of an obsession. I needed to use that to my advantage.

But could I do it? Could I fight my repulsion, my disgust, and my anger to make him believe that everything I'd said tonight wasn't true?

He'd see right through me. He'd know I was lying. But would it matter? Was he morally bankrupt enough to not care why he had my devotion as long as he had it?

Something told me soothing his pride would go a long way. It was the only chance I had, and I knew I had to take it.

When I came out of the shower wrapped in a towel, Bea had the burgundy dress hanging on the linen closet door with a lace bra and panties in the same color laid out on the vanity counter. A pair of silver stiletto sandals sat on the floor beneath the dress, and a full collection of my usual make-up and cosmetic items sat ready on the counter, an eerie glimpse into how thoroughly Emmett had been in cataloging my life.

As much as I was willing to give my life for those I loved, I couldn't help but wonder what would happen to me. If I managed to soothe Victor's anger during the flight, would I have a chance to escape once we arrived on his island? If I escaped, would he come after me? Not likely, since he couldn't enter the country again once he'd departed. But that didn't mean he couldn't send someone to do his dirty work. I had no doubt his reach wouldn't be diminished by distance.

What was my other option then? Ride it out and hope his feelings for me waned? Would it be possible for me to return if he tired of me?

Or would he simply dispose of me when he was done? I didn't know the standard breakup procedure for someone who had no qualms about killing.

I put on the bra and panties, forcing myself not to consider how they might be removed, and I stood staring at the burgundy dress when Bea knocked again.

"Need help with the dress?" she asked as she entered, not even waiting for a response to her knock. "We don't have much longer, and he'll be waiting downstairs."

She pulled the dress from the hanger and unzipped it, and then she helped me put it over my head and shimmy it down my body before zipping it closed.

"You've no time for a blow-dry, so how about we do a nice braided up-do instead? Sit here and I'll start your hair while you apply your make-up."

I nodded and sat on the round padded stool she'd pulled from beneath the vanity counter.

"Must take hours to dry all this hair," she said with an appreciative smile, her hands running through my hair as deftly as any hairdresser's ever had. She had it braided and twisted around my head into a clever up-do before I'd even finished with my makeup. The sleek edginess had come with minimal effort, and I was so impressed I didn't hesitate to accept when she offered to finish my makeup. I watched her in the mirror as she worked, blending shadows and executing a perfect cat-eye. She hummed softly, and a lump formed in my throat at the thought of my own mother. Would I ever see her again?

"Do you have daughters?" I asked Bea, and she nodded but offered no details. "I thought you must. Either that, or you've spent time working in a salon. Maybe both."

She didn't respond.

A loud knock on the door behind me brought forth a smile from Bea as my heart began to pound again.

"It's time, my dear. Chin up," she said, tucking her knuckle beneath my chin to gently guide me. "He's quite smitten with you. I'd daresay if you play your cards right, you could probably get him to do most anything you wanted."

"All I want is for him to let Seth go and leave my family to live in peace."

Clucking her tongue, she released me and began to gather my cosmetics back into the bag, which she then added to the suitcase she had carefully repacked. "Come along now. Don't keep him waiting and stoke his anger."

She zipped the case closed and went to open the door, handing it off to the giant who stood waiting in the hall.

I took a deep breath and laid my hand on my stomach, hoping to quell the ever-present nausea. Squaring my shoulders, I walked toward my fate, my sense of dread so heavy that I might as well have been walking to the executioner.

More images of Amy and my parents came to mind, and I focused on their faces with every step. I would do this for them. I would make it work to keep them safe and to protect them from my mistakes. Seth's face floated before my eyes, and my step faltered, the narrow stiletto catching on the rug as my ankle gave way. My hand went out instinctively, and I latched onto the giant's arm to keep from going down. The muscles beneath my hand were rock-hard and solid, and though I murmured an apology for grabbing him, I left my hand there, using his strength to steady myself as we walked toward the next chapter of my impossible life.

SEVENTEEN

Victor stood at the bottom of the stairs talking with Ned and Franco, and they all turned as Bea cleared her throat.

His eyes swept over me, and his smile came easy, bringing forth an unwanted memory of another time when I'd come out in a similar dress, desiring his smile and his approval for much different reasons.

I released the giant's arm to grasp the railing and begin my descent down the stairs. Victor rushed to meet me before I was even halfway down, taking me in his arms as his smile widened.

"Thank you," he whispered against my ear. "You are the most beautiful woman in the world, and I am the luckiest man to hold you. I *will* make this up to you."

He planted a kiss just beneath my earlobe, and I shuddered in repulsion, which he must have mistaken for desire judging by the look in his eyes.

As he escorted me the rest of the way down the stairs with his arm firmly ensconced around my waist, he nodded his head toward Ned and Franco.

"Finally," Ned mumbled none too quietly as he followed Franco out the front door.

When we stepped outside, two black SUVs sat waiting. Two men I didn't remember seeing before got into the second vehicle as Ned held the back passenger door of the first one open and Franco made his way around to the driver's door.

The giant placed my suitcase in the back as Victor helped me into the back seat, and I struggled not to hyperventilate as the walls of the vehicle closed in around me and my freedom slipped farther away.

This time, Victor slid into the back seat next to me, his arm laid possessively across my thighs as his hand squeezed my knee and drew me closer to him. He turned his face toward me, his lips pursed and his eyes expectant, and I forced myself to grant him a kiss as I mentally repeated the names of my parents and my sister over and over again.

"I love you," he said, reaching to caress my cheek. "I hate that you look terrified right now, and I wish I could erase your fears. It's going to be all right. You'll see, sweetness. Just give me a chance."

I wanted to jerk my face away from his touch. I wanted to grasp at the door handle on the other side and jump from the vehicle. I wanted to headbutt him and jam my elbow into his crotch. But instead, I forced a smile and managed to bob my head in a quick nod, and then I turned away to look out the window, even though nothing of the dark night was visible through its tint.

When we reached the large gates at the entrance to the property, I expected Franco to turn left, taking us back the way Emmett had brought me when we came. Instead, we turned right, winding deeper into the neighborhood until there were no more houses or driveways at all, only trees.

My nerves were on high alert, tingling with fear and apprehension, and I struggled to sit still.

Victor's hand moved gently back and forth across my knee, his fingers stroking my skin and making it crawl.

I bit down on the inside of my lip, willing myself not to slap his hand away and bolt from the vehicle. The only way I could protect my family was for Victor to want to make me happy. Their best outcome depended on his generosity. To achieve that, I needed him feeling affectionate and warm toward me.

But, God, it wasn't easy. I was equal parts terrified and enraged, and to muster a smile for the person responsible for both took everything I had. I didn't know how I'd ever find a way to move beyond that and make him believe I wanted his touch.

Soon, we came out of the trees, and the bright lights ahead revealed several large hangars surrounding a center expanse of concrete. All the hangars were dark except the last one on the right. Light poured onto the concrete from inside the hangar, illuminating the nose of a propeller plane parked inside. A helicopter sat in front of the open hangar, and beyond it, a small jet sat waiting with a set of stairs leading up to its open door.

My varying levels of panic throughout the night were nothing compared to the near-hysteria I felt seeing the plane that would carry me away from my family and toward my imprisonment and possible death. My body tensed, and I held my breath to keep from crying out.

Once Franco had parked the SUV near the helicopter, he and Ned exited. Franco opened the back hatch to retrieve my suitcase, and Ned moved to open the back door for Victor and me.

"Give us just a moment," Victor said, pulling the door closed as Ned narrowed his eyes at me and frowned.

Victor cupped my face in his hand, and then he slid his fingers down to rest his palm on my neck as his thumb traced my jawline.

"I know this must be very hard for you," he said, his eyes searching mine and his voice barely above a whisper. "I'm sorry that I'm causing you stress and unpleasantness. That was never my desire. I lost my temper with you, something I swore to myself I'd never do, and I did and said things I never should have. You must understand that you are my very life. I could no more fly away and leave you behind than I could take my heart from my body and leave it here. I promise, you'll live a happy life with me. You will be loved, you will be cherished, and you will never want for anything."

"Other than my family," I whispered.

He frowned and moved to take my hands in his.

"Once we're settled, they can come and visit any time they'd like," he said, looking down at my hands and then lifting his gaze to smile at me. "I would very much like to meet them. To get to know them. I hope someday they can be my family, too."

I resisted the urge to tell him that would never happen. I didn't want my family anywhere near Victor or anyone connected to him.

Ned rapped on the window. "We need to get in the air, boss."

Victor muttered a swear as he glanced toward Ned, but then he turned and flashed me his most charming smile. "Are you ready to fly away with me?"

Nothing in me was ready to get on a plane with a killer and leave everything I knew behind, but I squared my shoulders and nodded.

He opened the door and stepped out as I slid across the seat and swung my legs around to the side, hoping I could exit without flashing my lace panties to Ned.

Victor placed his hands on my waist, lifting me out and setting me on the ground. He pressed his lips to mine, his hands roaming across my backside with a slight squeeze before he released me.

Ned stood behind Victor with his arms crossed, his contempt for me obvious in his steely glare.

The three of us began to walk toward the plane. Franco walked ahead of us with my suitcase, and the two men from the SUV behind us each pushed a large wooden crate on wheels. With each step, my trepidation grew. My heart pounded so loudly that I feared Ned and Victor would both hear it.

I couldn't get on that plane. Once I boarded, it was over. My life was done. I needed to think of a way out. Something, anything, to delay takeoff. I needed to buy more time in the hope that Tristan would somehow come through and be successful in his search. Maybe he'd even know how to find Seth.

Running was out of the question. It would be damned near impossible in the stiletto sandals I wore, but even if I'd been wearing sneakers, there was nowhere to go. The other hangars surrounding us were all closed and dark, and the well-lit expanse of concrete guaranteed I'd be running in the wide open with Victor and his men in close pursuit. My mind was all too eager to play out a scene of me getting shot in the back and falling face forward, and I quickly dismissed that thought and searched for a different option.

As we passed the open door that led into the hangar, I saw a restroom sign on the wall inside, and I seized the opportunity to buy a little time.

"I need to go the bathroom."

"Here we go again," Ned muttered.

"There's a restroom on the plane," Victor said, not slowing his stride in the least.

I stopped walking, pulling my hand from his. "I need to use the restroom now. *This* restroom. I don't feel well, and I'd like a modicum of privacy."

"Very well," Victor said with an exasperated sigh. "Go ahead but be quick about it. Ned, wait with Danielle while Franco and I touch base with the pilot to make sure we're set."

Ned cursed loudly. "C'mon, boss. She's playing you. Surely, you can see that. Why can't she just pee on the plane?"

Victor moved so quickly that I didn't know what was happening until he had Ned pinned against the wall of the hangar, his forearm against Ned's throat.

"Enough!" Victor spat out, their noses almost touching as Victor pressed Ned harder into the wall. "You seem to have forgotten who I am and who you are while I was away. You will not disrespect me or my wife, no matter how many years you've spent by my side. Do I make myself clear?"

Ned nodded in response to the reminder, raising his hands in surrender, and I released the breath I'd been holding, shocked again by the volatility of Victor's mood swings and the swiftness with which he turned to violence.

After releasing Ned, Victor took a step back, straightening the cuffs on his sleeves. He dipped his head toward his left shoulder and then his right, moaning quietly when his neck emitted a loud crack.

"Danielle, it's been a long night for everyone here," he said, looking beyond me toward the plane. "Go ahead and use the restroom. Have the privacy you need, but don't take a moment longer than is necessary. Ned, you will accompany my wife."

Victor turned to continue to the plane as I walked past Ned toward the hallway beneath the restroom sign. The men's room was the nearest door in the hallway, followed by a water fountain and then the women's. Beyond that, the short hallway dead-ended in another hallway which was dark.

I pressed my forearm against the bathroom door and turned to glare at Ned, who was right on my heels as though he intended to accompany me inside.

"I can take it alone from here," I said.

"Make it quick," he grumbled with disdain.

Even though the bathroom's light sensor triggered on with my entry, I bent to look beneath the stalls and ensure I was alone in the room. It was only when I stood upright that I realized the walls were white with a wide gray stripe.

EIGHTEEN

I gasped and leaned against the stall partition to brace myself. If Seth was being held in this building, then I had to find him and free him before I got on that plane. But how? Ned would be glued to my side the minute I walked out of the bathroom, and he would take me straight to Victor, who was likely already boarded and ready to take off.

Loud voices signaled a commotion in the hangar, and I cracked open the door just wide enough to peer out. Victor's men were gathered on the other side of the small propeller plane, their legs and feet visible beneath it. Ned had walked toward them, and I knew I didn't have a second to lose.

I eased the bathroom door open farther and slipped out toward the longer hallway, pausing for only a brief second as I deliberated which way to go. There were four doors if I turned left and three if I went right, and it wasn't likely Ned would give me enough time to search all of them before he came looking for me.

Going with the option that had the most doors, I ran to the first door on the left and found it locked. I laid my ear against the door and listened for any sound inside.

"Seth?" I kept my voice low, not daring to call out loud enough for Ned to hear me. "Are you there? Can you hear me?"

The second and third doors were also locked. The fourth door was ajar, and I pushed it open hesitantly. The light sensor illuminated the space immediately, revealing the table and chair I'd seen on Victor's phone, but no Seth. I rushed into the room and around the right side of the table, desperate for any sign that he'd been there.

Voices filled the hallway, and I froze. Victor was arguing with someone, and their voices were getting closer.

"Have Nicholas and Troy find the damned pilot," Victor yelled. "If he's still alive, tell him we have to get that plane in the air. Did you get in touch with Paulie?"

"He isn't answering his phone," Franco said. "You think this is all the cop?"

"Who else could it have been?" Victor yelled. "When I get my hands on him—"

They were so close now that I knew they'd be inside the room any minute. Frantic, I searched for a place to hide, settling on a large cabinet in the corner behind the door. I'd just rounded the other side of the table, praying the cabinet would be empty, when I nearly stumbled over a body lying on the floor.

An ear-piercing scream erupted from me as I gripped the table to keep from falling over the dead man. His neck was bent at an impossible angle, his glassy eyes staring up at me from above a necktie that had been pulled so tight his head seemed to bulge above it.

"Danielle!" Victor's arms were around me within seconds, his hand cradling my head into his chest as he led me toward the door.

In my desperation and shock, I clung to his shirt and squeezed my eyes shut, trying to block out the image of those lifeless, protruding eyes staring at me. I'd seen bodies when I was a reporter, but never so unexpected and never so connected to my own fate.

"Dammit!" Franco's voice stood out in a chorus of swears and protests as the men crowded around their fallen friend.

"Why is she in here?" Victor barked at Ned. "I told you not to let her out of your sight."

"I thought she was in the bathroom."

As the initial fright began to wear off and I comprehended who held me, I pushed at Victor's chest to separate myself from him, but his arms tightened their grip around me as he continued to berate Ned.

"You had one job," Victor growled. "What if he had still been in here? What if she had come in during the scuffle?"

"I got distracted with all of you yelling about the mechanic getting popped. She must have slipped out when I wasn't looking."

Shoving at Victor again, I managed to take a step back as he turned to yell at the men who stood looking down at their colleague's body.

"Why are you standing there gaping? Go find this son-of-a-bitch and bring him to me!"

A deafening explosion rocked the entire building, shaking it on its foundation as glass shattered in the distance.

The men took off running toward the hall that led out into the hangar and Victor motioned for Ned and me to stay as he and the others ventured out.

"Stay with Danielle." Victor took a step back, drawing closer to Ned as his eyes narrowed, his voice becoming a low growl. "And this time, do *not* let her out of your sight."

Ned looked none too happy being left behind. If looks could kill, I would have been as dead as Paulie Necktie.

I didn't care. Hope and fear battled inside me as I struggled to assemble the puzzle pieces in my mind. I was certain Seth had been held in that room, and evidently, he'd made his escape and was doing what he could to prevent Victor's departure. As elated as I was to think of him being free and possibly freeing me, I was also terrified that they would find him. Victor was every bit the dangerous man I'd heard described in that courtroom, and I knew there was no way he'd let Seth go unharmed now.

Ned paced the hallway as we listened to the shouts of the men outside, and when things got quiet and we could no longer hear anything, he moved to the entrance leading out to the hangar and peered out.

"C'mon. Stay right with me, would you?"

He leveled his gun as he looked left and right and then stepped forward.

I hesitated, none too eager to leave the relative safety of the hallway. "Wouldn't we be safer in here? I mean, it seems like all hell is breaking loose out there. We should just—"

Ned moved faster than I thought he was capable of, towering over me as he gripped my arm. He bent his head so close to mine that when he spoke, the spray of spittle hit my face. "I can't be of any help to my guys hiding out in here. If I've got to babysit you, I need to do it out there so I can see what's happening and provide some kind of backup. In here, I'm blind and useless. Now, come on. Try not to get yourself killed, okay?"

We stepped out into the hangar, and despite my aversion to the man, I tucked myself as close behind Ned's back as possible, my eyes searching for any hint of danger. Well, more danger than I was in already.

The red and orange glow of a raging fire lit up the night outside the hangar, and as Ned moved us across the back wall, eventually we could see the fiery remains of one of the SUVs.

Victor came around the corner and into the hangar, his eyes registering surprise when he saw us.

"Christ! Get her out of here. What the hell are you doing?"

"I was trying to see what was going on," Ned said. "Besides, it's not like he'd harm *her*. Hell, he's doing all this *because* of her!"

Franco came in not long after Victor. "No sign of the other SUV. He must have taken it and gone. And we still haven't found the pilot or the attendant. Do you think it's possible he took them with him?"

Victor pinched the bridge of his nose between his fingers, and then he clenched both fists and let out a roar of frustration. I shrank back against the wall, and both Ned and Franco stood to attention, their eyes wide and unblinking.

"So close. So damned close I can taste it." Victor closed his eyes and rubbed his thumb between his brows, his voice calm and steady, though its chilling tone was even more frightening than his roar. He spat on the ground and then looked at Franco, his top lip curling as he spoke. "He can't get past the gates. When they find him, have him brought to me."

One of the men yelled in the distance, and Franco whipped his head around and took off running.

Victor pulled his phone from his pocket and called someone. "I need a pilot as fast as you can send me one."

He stared at the ceiling, his mouth drawn in a tight line.

"Oh, I'm well aware of what time it is. But I need a pilot. Now. Wake someone up and get someone out here. Pronto."

He ended the call and walked to the edge of the hangar to stare at the burning vehicle. Ned moved to stand beside him, and I hung back, wishing I could disappear from the whole scene.

"Your deputy deserted you, Danielle," Victor called over his shoulder to me. "He ran off without you. I guess you were wrong about him. Again."

I tried to feel relief. To be grateful that Seth had gotten away. But my gut told me there was no way Seth had left without any regard for what would happen to me. His departure had to be part of a bigger plan. Otherwise, why would he have blown up the SUV and drawn them outside?

Victor's phone rang, and he looked to Ned as he pulled it from his pocket.

"Take a look around over there," Victor said, gesturing toward the back corner behind the propeller plane. "See if you can find the keys for the other hangars." He slid his finger across the screen to answer the call as he walked outside the hangar and into the night.

"Come on," Ned said as we walked around the front of the small plane. "Stay close."

Franco yelled Victor's name in the distance, and I looked back over my shoulder, worried they had found Seth. I ran into Ned's back, and then leaned around him to see why he had stopped.

I clamped my hand over my mouth to stifle the scream that rose in my throat, burying my face in Ned's back to shut out the image of the dead body in front of us. Now I knew why Victor and his men had gathered with such commotion on this side of the plane when I was in the restroom earlier.

Ned jerked me around in front of him and forced my head in the direction of the body as I squeezed my eyes shut.

"Open your eyes and take a good look at him." His grip tightened and he shook my chin. "Open them, damn it."

I did as he asked and immediately regretted it. The dead man was flung backwards across a large red toolbox, his eyes staring at me from his upside-down face as blood seeped from the bullet wound in his chest and turned his gray coveralls a deep burgundy.

"Take a good look at him. If it wasn't for you, he'd be alive. So would Paulie," he growled, his breath hot against my ear as he gripped my face even tighter, his fingers pinching my chin. "These men that died here tonight, that's on you. We'd already be in the air and gone if you hadn't delayed everything."

A fleeting pang of guilt stabbed me in the gut, but I closed my eyes and refused to let it settle there. "It's not my fault they chose this line of work."

"First of all, he was a flight mechanic. But more importantly, if you'd just gone along with the plans, there wouldn't have been a need for anyone to get hurt."

I jerked away from his grasp and turned my back on the body. "Well, I'm sorry that I didn't care to be kidnapped and taken against my will. I never asked to be included in these plans."

Ned shrugged and shook his head as he moved forward to search the man's pockets. "I don't know what Victor sees in you, that's for sure. Hopefully, he's right about the deputy being wise enough to be long gone. If not, you're likely to get both of them killed before it's all over with, and for what?"

Suddenly, the hoot of a barred owl rang out across the night. I gasped and ran outside the hangar.

"What?" Ned said as he moved in front of me, waving his gun left and right as he searched the area.

"It was, uh, nothing, I guess." I shrugged in an attempt not to give anything away, even though my heart pounded so loudly that it seemed deafening in my ears. "I just got spooked by that owl, that's all. I'm not accustomed to being around dead bodies like you are, okay? It's got me freaked out a little."

The owl called out again, and though the wooded areas nearby made it entirely possible that it actually was a feathered nocturnal bird, my heart knew differently. I'd grown up with someone who could imitate the call of the Florida barred owl perfectly. So well, in fact, that he'd won a ribbon for it in an FFA competition when we were in high school. Seth was letting me know he was still there. Letting me know to hang on a little bit longer.

NINETEEN

"I gotta find those keys. Let's go," Ned said, pulling on my arm to take me back inside.

Jerking my arm from his grasp, I stepped away from him, hoping that wherever Seth was, he could see me and know I was okay. "I want to stay out here."

"I don't care what you want," Ned said. "I'm supposed to be watching you and I need to be in there. Now, come on."

Begrudgingly, I started to oblige his request, but then I hesitated, my eyes searching the darkness for any sign of Seth, which was silly. It wasn't like he was going to pop out and wave at me. He'd sent me a signal, and I had to trust that he had a plan. I turned to follow Ned, but then movement from the left caught my eye.

Victor and his men were approaching, accompanied by a man in a pilot's uniform and a buxom flight attendant. The woman wrung her hands back and forth across her wrists, and my hand went to my own bandaged wrist in remembrance of what she must be feeling.

The pilot nodded to something Victor said, and then he and the woman continued on toward the plane with Franco and the other two guys as Victor veered in my direction.

"Where were they?" Ned asked.

"Troy heard noises inside one of the hangars and broke the lock to get inside. He found them tied and gagged."

My heart sank. Time would run out more quickly now that we could fly.

"Why would this idiot do that?" Ned asked. "He had to have known we would find them. Why not just kill them?"

"Because he's not a killer," I said, my gaze leveled at Victor.

"No?" Victor said with one brow raised. "The flight mechanic might beg to differ with you."

I glanced toward the body stretched across the toolbox, shuddering again at the emptiness in the eyes staring back at me.

Victor cocked his head to one side and frowned. "Your deputy killed Paulie, too. So, tell me, why is it okay for your beloved Seth to kill and not me? Where's your outrage? Where's your indignation?"

"If he killed someone, I'm sure it was in self-defense."

"With Paulie, maybe. But the mechanic? Not likely. The man wasn't even armed."

"He wouldn't have killed if he didn't have to. You had him beaten and tied up. He likely feared for his life. He was trying to escape."

"Oh, so that justifies it for you, eh? I'm trying to escape, too. Does that not mean anything?"

I stared at him in silence, unwilling to engage in a debate over the merits of life with someone who took it so casually.

His phone rang, and he shook his head at me with a strange chuckle and then looked to Ned. "Get her on the plane."

I opened my mouth to protest, but he had already walked away, engaged in his phone conversation.

"You heard him. Let's go," Ned said as he reached for me.

Panic welled inside me, and I stepped back. "No! I'm not getting on that plane."

Ned's sick grin twisted my insides. "Oh, you are. One way or another. Even if you have to be unconscious."

He came toward me, and I turned to run for the hallway. If Seth was out there, if he was watching, I'd only need to lock myself inside a room until he could figure out a way to find me.

Ned lunged after me, his huge hand clutching my arm and jerking me to him. He wrenched my wrist around behind my back, the bandage pressing into my raw wounds with the rough gesture.

"Listen here," Ned sneered as he pulled my body back against his and shoved his gun into my ribs. "I'm not Victor, and I'm tired of your insubordination, you stupid bitch."

Neither of us were aware that Victor had returned before he slammed the butt of his gun into the back of Ned's head. The big man slumped as he stumbled forward, and I scrambled to get out from under him so he wouldn't take me down with him.

Ned recovered quickly and spun on unsteady feet to face his attacker, waving his gun wildly. His eyes widened in surprise as Victor rushed forward to grab the front of Ned's shirt, shoving him against the propeller plane. Victor cocked his pistol and pressed it to Ned's temple as their eyes locked.

"I told you never to disrespect my wife," Victor growled, his voice vibrating with an eerie timbre.

"Vic, come on," Ned pleaded, his eyes squinting with pain, confusion, or fear. Maybe all three. "You know I'm only looking out for you. That's all I've ever done. Our whole lives, I've had your back, man. Since we were kids! I'm trying to look out for you now."

Victor released Ned and began to pace in a tight circle, his nostrils flaring, his eyes wild, and his teeth clenched so tightly that his lips puckered, turning almost white with the effort.

He looked like a man who'd been teetering on the edge far too long and had begun to fall over the brink, and the tension in the air was so thick I found it hard to breathe. An explosion felt imminent, and I didn't dare move or speak lest I be the spark that ignited it.

Ned must not have felt the same caution.

"What are you doing, Vic? And why? You could have been halfway to the Maldives by now, or a third, at least. You could finally be free—free from a prison cell, free from the family. You won the jackpot with this deal, and you have your whole life ahead of you. Why risk losing it all?"

Franco approached the hangar, his eyes wary as he took in the situation.

Victor's pacing stopped. "What now?"

"We found the other SUV. The deputy used it to block the runway."

Victor closed his eyes and set his thumb to stroking between his brows again.

"Well, figure out a way to move it because Tony just called to let me know we've got company coming through the front gate of the development. Lots of company."

"Shit. All right. We're on it."

Franco signaled to the other two men and the three of them took off running toward the runway as Victor lifted his head to stare at Ned.

"Let me go help them," Ned said. "I can hotwire it. We'll get it moved, and we'll be on the plane and out of here before the cops arrive."

Victor shifted his gaze to me, and his eyes seemed unnaturally dilated, as though some hold on sanity had broken.

"So, it seems your beloved Seth didn't abandon you after all. He must still be here, thinking somehow he's going to be the one who takes you home."

Ned took a step forward toward Victor. "Let him. You don't need her, and if you leave her behind, they may not even pursue us."

"I. Am. Not. Leaving. Here. Without. My. Wife." Victor ground out the words through clenched teeth with his eyes closed and his forehead scrunched so tightly it seemed as though speaking took a Herculean effort.

The distant sound of helicopters drew Ned's attention, and I began to search the sky for any sign of the cavalry's approach.

Ned looked back to Victor, whose eyes were still closed in his contorted face.

When Ned spoke, his voice was soft and consoling. "She doesn't want to be with you, man. She's gonna keep screwing things up until you let her go. She doesn't love you."

Victor's eyes opened, and the look he gave Ned should have made the man step back and keep his thoughts to himself.

Ned must have had a death wish, though, because he pushed the envelope further. "She's not right for you. She messed with your head right from the start, and you haven't been thinking clearly since you met her."

I opened my mouth to defend myself, but thought better of it and promptly closed it. I didn't want to draw any more attention than necessary, especially since it appeared Victor was actually considering Ned's words. If Ned convinced him I was expendable, my situation would become even more precarious, something I hadn't thought possible given its already dire state.

Ned laid his hand on Victor's shoulder, and Victor turned his head to stare down at Ned's hand.

"C'mon," Ned whispered, giving Victor a gentle shake. "There'll be plenty of other women in the islands. They'll be falling all over you like they always have. You'll forget this bitch in no time."

In a split second, Ned went from leaning toward Victor with a conspiratorial grin to lying flat on his back with a bullet hole in his forehead and a pool of blood seeping from the back of his skull.

Pain stabbed through my ears with the deafening explosion of the gun firing so close to me, leaving them ringing with a shrill, high-pitched whine.

Victor turned to me immediately, his expression horrorstricken.

"Oh God, Danielle, I'm sorry," Victor said, his voice pleading, but then almost instantly, his face turned angry again. "Christ, will nothing go right? Please stop screaming!"

Until he said it, I hadn't known that I was, and I clamped my hand over my mouth in an attempt to quiet the involuntary reaction.

Victor rushed forward, his arms lifted like he meant to hold me, and I backed farther away as I screeched, "Don't touch me!"

"I'm sorry," he repeated. "I lost my temper. He pushed me too far."

"You shot him for nothing," I choked out, my voice a gurgle as fear constricted my throat.

"Yes, I shot him, but not for nothing!" His anger had flared again, and his wild eyes widened even more beneath raised eyebrows. "For you! I told you I'd do anything for you, and apparently, that includes severing ties with someone I've known since childhood because he insulted you."

"Severing ties? You killed him!" I shook my head to dispel the replay of it that seemed to be on a continuous loop in my mind. "You didn't do this for me. I never asked you to kill anyone."

He ran his fingers through his hair and swore. "No, this is true. You did not. Ned caused his own death with his disrespect."

"Since when is calling someone a bitch a death sentence?"

My eyes spied Ned's gun where it had fallen to the floor, and I tried to calculate how long it would take me to reach it.

"It's not like I didn't warn him! I was defending *you!*" Victor raised his hands in frustration and looked toward the ceiling as he turned from me just enough to give me a window of opportunity.

I reached down to scoop up Ned's gun, releasing the safety as I leveled it at Victor.

His eyes darkened as he stared at me, and his upper lip began to twitch along with that overworked muscle in his jaw.

"Danielle, don't do anything you'll regret." His voice was cold steel.

"I've had enough regrets in the past two years to last me a lifetime. I'm done regretting. I'm taking back control of my life, and I intend to live it fully without looking over my shoulder and without needing a bottle to numb it."

He stepped toward me, and I stepped back, my hands trembling on the gun as I cocked it. It had been years since I'd held one. Tenth grade. Maybe eleventh. Seth and his brother Noah had taught me to shoot at targets in the backyard when we were kids, and I'd always been damned good at it. But I'd never dreamed I would have a human being in my sights, and I wondered if I'd have the courage to pull the trigger.

The fact that I'd cocked it seemed to convince Victor I was at least considering it, and his attitude shifted almost immediately. He lifted both hands in surrender, even though his left hand still held his pistol. His gaze softened, and so did his voice.

"I understand that you're upset. I've broken another promise to you, haven't I? I swore I was done with that life, and I thought I was."

The quiet repentance in his voice and the sudden calmness in his demeanor brought to mind Jekyll & Hyde, and I braced my stance and held the gun as steady as I could, watching for any sign of the monster's return.

He let his hands drop to his sides, and a frown clouded his face. "I was certain I had pulled my last trigger, and yet, in the downward spiral of our circumstances, I find myself in survival mode, relying on my instincts and doing what comes naturally."

Killing came naturally for him. It always would. No matter what promises he made, there would be no reform for a man whose base instincts were to react in rage and violence.

"Please forgive me. I'll do better, I swear. I just need to get us away from here. I need to know you're safe, that we're safe. I swear it will be different then." He extended his right hand toward me as he stepped closer. "Give me the gun."

"No. Stay where you are." My voice shook as badly as my hands.

"You won't shoot me," Victor said, his lips spreading in a maddening grin. "You don't have it in you to be a killer. You're not like me or my men. Or Seth."

"Seth is not a killer," I said, shaking my head.

Victor chuckled. "I've never understood this obsession with him. It was a childhood romance. He didn't care enough to carry it into adulthood. So why is it that you cling to this ridiculous notion you have of him?"

The whirring of the helicopters grew louder as they got closer, and as Victor glanced toward the sky, I made the mistake of doing the same.

He lunged, and I retreated to find my back against the small plane. I had nowhere to go. I'd either have to shoot him or stand down, and I didn't want to do either.

"Don't come any closer, or I will shoot you."

"No, you won't." The grin he flashed was his most charming. The one that had done me in and gotten me in this mess two years earlier. "If you were going to do it, you already would have. You don't want to shoot me. You're too tenderhearted. You don't have what it takes to pull the trigger."

"She doesn't have to," Seth said, entering the hangar from the other side with a gun trained on Victor. "I'll pull it for her."

TWENTY

Relief washed over me, and my limbs damned near went to jelly.

Victor spun around immediately, taking aim at Seth, but then, he shifted so he could swing his head back and forth, watching us both. His gun remained on Seth, though.

Seth's eyes never left Victor's, but his questions were directed at me.

"Are you okay? Did he hurt you?"

"I'm fine," I said, resisting the urge to run across the hangar and throw my arms around him.

"Your concern is touching," Victor said, "but I wouldn't hurt my own wife."

"She's not your wife," Seth said. "And if you call her that one more time, the SWAT team that's on its way here right now will find your corpse when they arrive."

"You won't shoot me either." Victor's grin was lethal this time, not charming. "You're too duty-bound. Honor and all that. I bet the only way you'll shoot is self-defense."

Seth chuckled. "I wouldn't be so sure about that. I would have killed you for what you'd done to her even before you showed up tonight."

Victor lifted an eyebrow and his grin widened. "Ah. Danielle, perhaps you don't know your white knight as well you believe."

"Dani, I need you to hide," Seth said, his gaze unwavering as he smiled back at Victor. "Shit's about to get crazy here from the land and the sky, and I want you to find someplace to lay low and wait it out. You don't come out until you're certain it's safe, you hear me?"

My heart leapt to my throat at the thought of being separated again when we'd just been reunited. "I don't want to leave you. I want to stay with you. We'll be safe once they get here. Let me stay with you."

Suddenly, Franco pulled up to the front of the hangar in the recovered SUV. His eyes widened as he took in the scene before him, and then Seth yelled, "Now, Dani! Run! Hide!"

Franco accelerated, driving straight toward Seth, and nearly taking me out in the process. I scrambled out of his path and around the front of the plane as gunfire echoed throughout the hangar. With no time to search for options, I flung open the only door I could see and began to climb the staircase behind it without much consideration for where it might lead. My heel caught in the metal grate of a step, and as I cursed the stiletto sandals for the hundredth time since I'd put them on, I slipped them off and continued up the stairs barefooted, wincing at the sharp metal pressing into the soft undersides of my feet.

More bursts of gunfire rang out, and I instinctively ducked and then ran faster. With each shot fired off from the hangar below, I flinched, worried that Seth had been hit. When I reached the landing at the top, a window offered a view outside, and the helicopters were clearly visible in the lightening pre-dawn sky. We just had to survive a few minutes longer, and the cavalry would arrive.

I looked down at the ground outside the window. One of Victor's men was running from the plane toward the hangar. He stopped and aimed his gun. Then with the sound of another bullet being fired, he dropped, and I took that as a sign that Seth was unharmed enough to still be shooting back.

Flinging open the door on the top landing, I rushed out onto a metal catwalk that spanned the expanse of the building to a door on the other side. From my vantage point, I could see the entire hangar below, but not Seth or Victor. It seemed the battle had stopped for a moment. I strained to hear any movement beneath me, but the incessant ringing in my ears and the sound of the approaching helicopters made it impossible to even hear my own thoughts.

Desperate for any sign of Seth, I inched farther out onto the catwalk, moving slowly so I wouldn't draw attention to my presence. The helicopters were so close now that I could feel the reverberation of their whirring rotors in my chest.

Somewhere behind me outside the hangar, the rapid bursts of an automatic rifle ripped through the air, and though they weren't shooting at me, I dropped as low as I could, holding onto the rails for dear life in my vulnerable and exposed position. A new fear gripped me at the thought of them taking out the helicopters and preventing the cavalry's arrival. If they were to succeed in bringing one of the big birds down, who knew where it might end up, and the last place I wanted to be was suspended on a piece of scaffolding high above the concrete floor. The door on the other side offered refuge, so I scurried over the catwalk, praying no one would see me.

A booming voice filled the air as someone on the helicopter demanded that those on the ground drop their weapons, but based on the answering round of shots, the request wasn't heeded.

As I reached for the door handle, I made eye contact with Franco down below in his hiding space behind the toolbox with the body on it. I held his gaze as I pulled the door open, turning too late to prevent a crash into the arms of the one person I most wanted to hide from.

Victor wrapped me in a painfully tight embrace, shoving me up against the door with my arms pinned at my sides. "Well, hello, sweetness. So nice to have you back where you belong."

He moved to kiss me, and I headbutted him with all my strength, the world going black and then bursting with bright flashes as the pain exploded behind my eyes.

"Dammit," Victor growled, but he didn't release me. "Why are you making this so difficult?"

"Because you're forcing me to do something I don't want to do! Why can't you just let me go? You swore to me tonight that you were the man I fell in love with, and I'm begging that man to let me go. Be the decent person I know you can be. It's not too late for you to do the right thing."

"Getting us out of here is the right thing! As soon as we're in the air, as soon as I know you're safe, I've already sworn to you I will leave this way of life behind."

My mouth dropped open. "Do you not hear those helicopters? Seth said a SWAT team is on its way. There's no way in hell they will let you take off. It's done, Vic. It's over."

"No." He shook his head. "We vowed until death do us part. As long as we're both still breathing, you're still my wife, and we still have a chance."

"I told you what would happen if you called her that again," Seth said from the other end of the catwalk as he walked toward us with his gun drawn.

In the next moment, it was as though the earth had slowed its crawl, suspending time so that everything unfolded in slow motion.

From the corner of my eye, I saw Franco move to stand, his arms lifting as he aimed his gun at Seth. Detecting the movement below, Seth turned to face him just as Victor moved forward, shoving me behind him to take aim at Seth as well.

It was pure instinct that drove me to raise Ned's gun and pull the trigger. I didn't have time to think about what I was doing or whether it was right or wrong. I was simply consumed by the need to make sure Seth survived.

Four shots rang out from four guns in almost perfect synchronic-ity. Victor and Franco both went down, and Ned's gun fell from my hand as I stared at the motionless body of the man I'd married. The man I'd shot.

Tiny needles prickled across the palm of my hand from the force of the gun's discharge, and I clutched my fist to my chest, slumping to my knees in shock. I tried to tear my eyes from the gaping hole in Victor's back, but they wouldn't obey.

Then the world sped back up, and I clung to the railing as the catwalk seemed to sway and the edges of my vision began to go black.

Something moved on the other end of the catwalk, and I managed to focus once I saw it was Seth. My heart rejoiced to see that he was upright and breathing. He stood at an angle, looking down as he scanned the hangar for any further threats, and when he turned, panic overtook me as I watched the dark red stain rapidly spreading across his shoulder.

Intent on reaching Seth, I struggled to crawl past Victor on the narrow surface, cringing as my body made contact with his. My stomach heaved, but I bit down hard on my lip and kept moving forward as Seth walked toward me, but then he turned back to look outside the building.

I shut my eyes briefly and allowed myself to take a breath once I was clear of Victor's body, but just as I drew the air in, his hand shot out and grasped my ankle, his fingers clamping down as he sought to hold onto me. My reaction was automatic. I kicked with every bit of force I could muster, drawing on the panicked adrenaline coursing through me. The heel of my foot made contact with Victor's shoulder, the impact strong enough to push his weakened body over the edge beneath the rail.

He fell to the concrete below with a sickening thud so loud it drowned out the ringing of my ears and shook me to my core. I held tightly to the railing and stared down at his body in horror, and though I opened my mouth to scream, nothing would come out.

And then, Seth was there, his arms wrapped around me as he turned my head toward his chest and crooned in my ear.

"Don't look. It's okay. You're okay."

"I killed him," I whispered as I twisted my fists into his shirt.

"It's okay."

"It's not okay!" Tears sprang forth as I shuddered. "Oh, my God. I killed him."

Seth cradled my face in his hands, pressing his forehead to mine as our gazes locked.

"Listen to me! You did what you had to do. You saved my life."

Someone yelled from outside, and I jerked at the sound, on full alert again. Men in black entered the hangar below, scurrying beneath us like ants.

"Look at me," Seth called, bringing my attention back to him, which brought my eyes back to his shoulder.

"You've been shot! You're bleeding."

He glanced down at his shoulder and then pulled me closer against his chest. "I'm fine. It's nothing. The bullet grazed me and kept going."

Tristan's voice rang out from below.

"Hey! You two all right up there?"

"Yeah," Seth called down. "It's about time you showed up."

A new fear struck me as the reality of what I'd done sank in.

"What are they going to do to me?"

He held me tighter, pressing his lips to the top of my head. "Nothing, baby. Nothing at all. Don't worry, okay? It's going to be all right. You did what you had to do."

A flurry of activity bustled beneath us, and I wrapped my arms around his waist and buried my head in his chest, squeezing my eyes shut against it all.

He winced and sucked in a breath as his hands slid down my arms, pulling them from his waist.

I pulled back to look up at him. "Are you okay?"

"Yeah, I'm fine. I think I may have a couple of cracked ribs."

"From the...when they...at the hotel?"

Seth gave a half shrug. "Maybe, but then I had a run-in with a guy swinging a wrench. But I'm fine. Don't worry about me. I need to get us downstairs, though. Can you stand?"

I nodded, and he helped me up, cautioning me as he did so. "Don't look down, okay? Just keep your eyes on the door. I'm with you every step of the way."

The initial shock had begun to wear off, but the room still went sideways when I stood.

Seth's strong arms were around me in an instant. "I've got you."

"I'm okay. Just a little dizzy." I focused on the door ahead of me, trying to ignore everything else.

We made our way downstairs, and as we exited into the hangar, I couldn't help looking over at Victor's body, lying crumpled on the concrete surrounded by a dark pool of blood.

I shuddered again and closed my eyes, but the image remained, impossible to escape. A tidal wave of nausea hit me, and I doubled over and emptied the meager contents of my stomach.

"Can we get her some water?" Seth called out, rubbing his hand across my back.

"On it," a voice responded as I spit and wiped the back of my shaking hand across my mouth.

"You okay?" Seth asked, his voice close to my ear.

I closed my eyes and nodded, and then I forced myself to stand upright, taking it slowly in case the room tilted on me again.

"I'm fine," I said, though I was anything but.

"Let's get you outside for some fresh air."

As Seth led me past the vomit on the floor, Tristan walked up to us, his gray eyes filled with concern.

"Are you all right, Dani?"

I nodded and laid my hand across my stomach to ease it. "Yeah. I will be. A little overwhelmed, I think. It's been a rough night, to say the least. Thank you for, um, coming."

"Of course," he said with a tip of his head.

"Took you long enough," Seth said.

"I was trying, man. Damned red tape and bureaucracy took

forever with deciding whose jurisdiction it was and what warrants were needed. Then, when you called and the location changed from the house to the airstrip, that threw everything for a loop."

"Were you at the house, too?" I asked Seth, my eyes wide with surprise.

"No. They brought me straight here."

"So, how did you know where the house was?"

"He didn't," Tristan said. "We'd already gotten a call from the house before Seth was able to contact me from the airstrip."

I shook my head in confusion. "A call? From whom?"

"I'm, er, not at liberty to say. It seems the owners of that house have been on the radar for some time, so we have an undercover agent in place there. Concern for your well-being prompted a call to a superior officer, and that set the wheels in motion faster than I could get them moving."

"Bea," I said with absolute certainty.

Tristan shrugged. "I honestly don't know."

"I do. I have no doubt it was her."

Turning his focus to Seth, Tristan frowned. "You gonna have them take a look at that shoulder, or are you trying to look macho by standing there bleeding?"

"It's just a graze."

"C'mon, tough guy," Tristan said with a grin, and he led us toward the paramedics outside.

As we left the hangar, I couldn't help glancing over my shoulder, even though I didn't want to see Victor's body again. They'd covered him with a black tarp, but my stomach flipped on itself just the same.

He'd loved me. He'd wanted to spend the rest of his life with me, but I'd taken his life instead. I'd killed him. I was a murderer just like he was.

Seth reached for my hand, tugging my attention back to him. "Hey, look at me. I know this is hard for you. It's never an easy thing to take a life, regardless of the circumstances. But I meant what I said before. You did what you had to do. You saved my life."

It didn't surprise me that Seth knew what I was thinking or where my mind had gone. He'd always been able to read me like a book.

"I know. I just hate that I had to end his to do it. Why wouldn't he just leave? He could have been long gone. He'd still be alive. So would everyone else here. Why couldn't he just walk away?"

Seth frowned and glanced back at Victor before wrapping his arm around my shoulders and pulling me forward with him. "Because in his dark, obsessed, and unhealthy way, he loved you."

"And I killed him for it."

"C'mon, babe. Don't do that to yourself. What would he have done if you hadn't stopped him?"

I took a deep breath and blinked back my tears. "He would have killed you. And he would have taken me or died trying once these guys arrived. I know that, but it doesn't make it any easier. I feel horrible that I caused all this death and that everyone was scrambling to rescue me."

"You didn't cause any of it. It's not like you called this guy up and asked him to come get you. The decisions he made set him on a path to die tonight, and while I hate it was at your hand, it wasn't your fault. He had choices. Those other men? They had choices, too. No one had to die here tonight. That's not on you."

A paramedic approached us, and by the time Seth had been examined and we'd both answered all the necessary questions and given our statements, the sun was well on its way up into the sky.

"Are these yours?" Seth asked as he walked toward me holding the stiletto sandals.

"No. I mean, yes, I was wearing them, but they're not mine." I looked down at the burgundy dress and wished I could rip it from my skin. "Neither is this dress. Victor made me wear this because there was someone he was meeting. Someone he said he wanted to impress."

"Someone he was selling crates of guns to, according to the pilot and Victor's guy on the plane." He cocked his head to one side, and his brow furrowed. "How are you feeling?"

"Hmm. What's the word to describe when you've been up for, like, twenty-four hours, and you got drunk, and then got scared sober, and then had to run for your life, and then got kidnapped and tied up, and then got forced to shower and dress up, and then saw dead people and dodged bullets, and then..." My voice failed, unable to apply my sad attempt at humor to the fact that I'd taken Victor's life. "Crappy. Let's just say I feel pretty crappy."

"Well, I was gonna ask if you wanted breakfast, but probably not, huh?"

"I thought you were supposed to go to the hospital to make sure you don't have a concussion and to get your ribs checked. I heard you tell the paramedics that it wasn't necessary for them to take you and that you'd go on your own."

He grinned. "You heard that, did ya? All right, but they didn't say I couldn't get breakfast first. Unless...you're not hungry? If you don't want to—"

"You know, now that you mention it, I'm actually really hungry. We can get breakfast, as long as you agree to let me drive you to the hospital afterwards."

"Deal, but I'm driving."

"No, you're not! You likely have a concussion, you probably have broken ribs, and you've been shot. I'm driving."

To my surprise, he didn't argue, and we walked in silence to my car, which had been found in the hangar next to the one we were in.

Seth went to the driver's door and held it open for me, and I paused to look up at him before I got in.

"Thanks," I whispered, wishing there was a stronger word to convey my gratitude for all he'd done for me and endured for me.

Smiling, he reached to tuck back a section of my hair that had worked its way free from Bea's braids.

"I'll take a bullet for you anytime, D," he said with a wink.

"I hope there's never another occasion where that might be needed."

"Me too, but I'd be willing, just the same." He began to draw in a deep breath, but then he grimaced and laid his hand over his side. "Damn. Remind me not to do that again."

"We should get you to a hospital."

"Unfortunately, there's not really much they can do for ribs."

"Still, you need to get checked out."

"I will, but before we go, I need to tell you something, and I don't want to put it off any longer. It's something I should have said earlier tonight, but I guess I'm just a damned coward."

"Coward?" I raised my eyebrows with a scoffing laugh. "You just took on the Mafia all by yourself. I don't think anyone would call you a coward. And why on earth did you do that, by the way? I can't believe you stuck around. I mean, once you got in that SUV, why didn't you just take off and get out of here?"

"And leave my girl behind? Not a chance."

"But you could have been killed."

"Well, I wasn't, but I did have plenty of time to think I might be, and here's what I know." He laid his hand on the side of my neck, his thumb stroking my skin and sending goosebumps rippling all over me. "I love you, Dani. I've never stopped loving you. I was a damned fool to let you go."

I smiled, my heart swelling until it felt it might burst. "I love you, too, and I'm so sorry I—"

He pressed his finger to my lips. "Don't. We can't keep apologizing for the past, and we can't go back and change it. A couple of times tonight, it looked like I might not have a future, and especially not one that had you in it. Now, you probably think I'm talking crazy after everything's that happened, but...I want a future with you. I want you in my life."

My smile grew wider as I stretched up on my toes to press my lips against his.

"You've got me."

"And I want you to know that I've thought about it a lot, and I'm willing to go with you. You don't even have to tell me where we're going. It doesn't matter."

"Go?" My brows scrunched in confusion. "Go where? What are you talking about?"

His confusion mirrored mine. "I just, um, assumed you'd probably want to go back to Chicago. Or if your memories there are screwed up now, some other big city. Somewhere you can pursue your career and do all the things you wanted."

I ran my hand up his chest and over his uninjured shoulder to curl my fingers around the back of his neck. "I don't need to go anywhere anymore. Everyone I love is in Cedar Creek. It's my home, and it's where I belong. With you is where I belong."

He bent his head to kiss me, his mouth claiming mine as his hand slid down my back and pulled me firmly against him.

My heart quickened as though it was awakening after a long slumber, and suddenly, nothing in me felt numb anymore.

EPILOGUE

I lowered my sunglasses as I watched Seth and Tristan stand together by the grill in Tristan's backyard. The lake shimmered in the distance, the deep orange of the setting sun making the water look like it was ablaze. The smell of hamburgers cooking wafted up to the deck, and I smiled in contentment.

"My fiancé sure does make a handsome chef, doesn't he?" Sloane asked as she lounged in the chair next to me. "You ready for another Jameson?"

"No, I'm good." I rattled the ice cubes in the glass.

She lifted an eyebrow with a grin. "Since when do you stop at one?"

I shrugged and look back toward Seth. "I actually haven't been drinking all that much since, you know, that night. I'd been using it to escape my life, and now, my life isn't something I want to escape anymore."

Sloane sighed. "I'm so relieved they finally cleared you. I mean, I knew they would. Obviously, it was self-defense, whether you shot him in the back or not. He would have killed Seth and kidnapped you if you hadn't stopped him. It's ridiculous that you even had to go through all that interrogation."

"No, they had to investigate. I'm just glad it's over." Laying back against the chair, I closed my eyes to block out the memories.

"All of it, right? Tristan said their intel seems pretty certain the Mafia won't retaliate since Victor had already gone rogue against them. You're free, and you're safe. That crazy chapter in your life is over, and from the looks of things, the next chapter will be a happy one."

"God, I hope so. I'd just take normal at this point, but yeah." I opened my eyes and gazed at Seth, who glanced over at me and smiled as though he could feel my stare. "Things are definitely looking good. I'm the happiest I've been in a very long time."

My phone rang, and I sat up straight when I saw it was my sister.

"Is it time?" I asked, not even bothering to say hello.

"Yep. My water broke," Amy said. "We're on our way to the hospital now. Meet me there?"

"Of course. I'll be right there." I looked to Sloane, who was grinning from ear to ear.

"You're going to be an aunt!"

"I'm gonna be an aunt! Oh, my gosh. We've got to go. Seth! It's time!"

I stood as Seth said goodbye to Tristan and walked toward the porch. "I'm so sorry, Sloane. I hate to skip out on dinner, but—"

"Don't be ridiculous," she said with a laugh. "It's not every day you welcome a niece into the world. We can grill hamburgers any time."

She was right. I wasn't going anywhere. This was home. This was my life. Seth and I could get together with our friends whenever we wanted.

I hugged Sloane and then gathered my purse as Seth told her goodbye.

We'd just rounded the corner of their house when a car pulled up the drive and parked behind Seth's truck.

"We need to get out," Seth called to the driver as the man opened his door. "We're in a bit of a hurry."

"This will only take a moment," the man said. "Are you Danielle Ward?"

I looked at Seth before nodding. "Yes, I am. Who are you?"

"I'm Wallace Bradford. I have a delivery for you that needs to be signed for." He held up a large white envelope.

"A delivery? What delivery?"

Seth stood by my side as the man approached me.

"You mentioned you're in a hurry, so we can talk later. I'll give you some time to review the papers before we discuss the particulars."

He handed me a clipboard with a paper attached and pointed to indicate where I should sign.

I didn't even bother looking at the papers. "I'm not signing anything unless you tell me what's going on."

"What's this about?" Seth asked, his body tensing next to me.

"I am an attorney in the employ of Victor Gallo."

A feeling of dread punched me in the gut, and I reached to lay my hand on Seth's arm. He took my hand in his as the man continued.

"Mr. Gallo had made financial arrangements to provide for you in the event of his death."

I shook my head, handing him back the clipboard.

"No. I want nothing to do with that. I don't need his money."

The man cocked his head to one side. "Be that as it may, you were his legal beneficiary."

"That can't be. We were divorced, um, prior to his death."

"I'm well aware. But the fact remains that Mr. Gallo wished for you to be provided for—quite well, I might add—in the event of his death. I assure you it was still his intention right up until his untimely end."

I looked to Seth, who looked as though he was about to punch the man.

"Ms. Ward, I can understand your hesitation, but I would encourage you to at least take some time to look over the documents before you make any decisions. It's not a paltry sum we're discussing. Perhaps if you don't want to benefit personally, you might have a cause you could funnel the money toward."

My mind spun with the unexpected news. "I don't understand. I was under the impression that Victor's assets were seized."

"Yes, but this was an inheritance from his late mother. It wasn't attached to his, shall we say, other business interests, in any way. These funds were placed in a separate account at the time of her death, and they've not been touched. They've been there accruing interest, and when you and Mr. Gallo met, he added your name to the account as his sole beneficiary. I assumed you knew all this."

"No. I wasn't aware."

"We need to go," Seth said. "As I said before, we're in a bit of a hurry."

Mr. Bradford gave one quick nod. "Yes, of course. I won't keep you. Ms. Ward, your signature will only confirm that you've received the paperwork. It will in no way obligate you one way or another with the funds. Regardless of your feelings on the matter, you *are* Mr. Gallo's sole heir, and therefore, at some point, you will need to make a decision as to how you wish to proceed."

He offered the clipboard again, and after reading to verify what I was signing, I scrawled my name across the bottom. He handed me the envelope and then pulled a business card from a holder in his pocket.

"Here's my number. Look over the papers and see what's at stake. Take your time. Think about all the possibilities. And then give me a call when you've made your decision. I've already been well compensated to handle matters in whatever manner you choose."

I stared down at the envelope with my name printed on the front as Mr. Bradford turned and walked back to his car.

"Wait," I called to him. "How did you find me?"

"When no one answered at your listed residence, I asked around in town. They told me you were often in the company of your business partner, Ms. Reid, and they told me where to find her. There's something to be said for small town life, I suppose. Let's talk soon."

I flipped through the papers as Seth drove us to the hospital, my jaw dropping as I counted the zeroes in the account balance.

"What should I do?" I asked Seth once I'd read the numbers off to him. "I should refuse it, right?"

"Well, from what he said, it's not a matter of *refusing* it, babe. Legally, it's already yours. It comes down to what you want to do with it. That's a lot of money. With money like that, you could build your own theater. You could build your own house. Hell, you could build a town."

"But it's Victor's money."

"It was Victor's money. He left it to you. Like it or not, you *were* married to him. So, it makes sense that he would have listed you as the beneficiary."

"The attorney did say it wasn't Mafia money, right?"

Seth shrugged. "He said it was an inheritance from Victor's mother. Who knows what her ties were to the family business! But it's possible that money is clean, I suppose."

I tapped my fingers against my lip as I stared at the number again. "If I don't accept this, what happens to it?"

"That's a question for the attorney, D. I honestly don't know."

"This is a shit ton of money. I could...I could do so much."

"You could. You could even give it all away if you wanted. Then, no matter where the money came from, you could turn it into something good."

I shoved the papers back into the envelope and tossed it on the dash.

"He said I have time to decide, so I don't have to think about this right now. I have more important things to think about than money. My sister is having my niece any minute now, and the man I love is by my side to help me welcome her into the world. To welcome her home to Cedar Creek. Nothing else matters."

Try as I might, I couldn't stop thinking about the money and all the things it could do. For my family. For the theater Sloane and I wanted to create. For the community. For whatever causes I chose to involve myself with.

I still had my reservations, of course, but Seth was right. I had the opportunity to take something bad and make something good.

In the bourbon world, they fill the barrel knowing they'll lose some of the precious liquid in the aging process. The portion that evaporates is called the angel's cut. The portion that seeps into the barrel is the devil's due. What's left behind is the good stuff.

I'd made some stupid choices in my life, and in many ways, I felt I'd already paid the devil his due. But I'd had some prayers answered along the way, so it seemed only fair that I give the angels their cut and help out others if I was able. And as for me?

Well, I had my family back. I had my home. I had Seth.

I smiled as I took his hand in mine, knowing that what lay ahead was the good stuff.

Want to know what Seth was doing after Dani left the motel? Sign up for Violet's monthly newsletter at BookHip.com/RQFQTL and receive bonus chapters from Seth's point of view.

Want to spend more time in Cedar Creek? Check out Cedar Creek Mysteries or Cedar Creek Families!

CEDAR CREEK

WANT MORE IN CEDAR CREEK?

Welcome to the small town of Cedar Creek! This quaint community is home to a collection of recurring characters who interact from book to book. If you've enjoyed reading Volume 1 in Cedar Creek Suspense, check out Cedar Creek Mysteries and Cedar Creek Families. They both feature stories of love, laughter, family, & friendships, but the mysteries have the added elements of suspense, mystery, and a ghost or two! To find out more, visit www.violethowe.com.

ALSO BY VIOLET HOWE

<u>Tales Behind the Veils</u>

Diary of a Single Wedding Planner

Diary of a Wedding Planner in Love

Diary of an Engaged Wedding Planner

Maggie

<u>The Cedar Creek Collection</u>

Cedar Creek Mysteries:

The Ghost in the Curve

The Glow in the Woods

The Phantom in the Footlights

Cedar Creek Families:

Building Fences

Crossing Paths

Cedar Creek Suspense:

Whiskey Flight

<u>Soul Sisters at Cedar Mountain Lodge</u>

Christmas Sisters

Christmas Hope

Visit www.violethowe.com to subscribe to Violet's monthly newsletter for news on upcoming releases, events, sales, and other tidbits.

ACKNOWLEDGMENTS

Bonnie, Teresa, Tawdra, Lisa, Melissa, & Cathy: Thanks for continuing to be my sounding board, my voices of reason and plausibility, and my extra eyes. With helicopters this time.

Greg: Thanks for the formal bourbon lesson and thorough tasting demonstration. I appreciated you sharing your knowledge and experience, especially that part about the angel's share and devil's cut. I knew as soon as you said it that would make it on these pages somehow.

Robbie, Char, Teri, & Sarah: Thanks for being willing to be a part of my education. There's no sacrifice too great for friendship, right? Twelve bottles later, and we're all still standing.

Logan: Thanks for not blowing up the house as a kid, and thanks for helping me research what might be on hand in an airport hangar to create just the explosion my hero needed under just the right circumstances.

Ari: Thanks again for the legal terminology and the support in determining what I could put these characters through.

Michael: Thanks for being Tristan and Levi's back-up and a wealth of information on a deputy's resources and procedures.

ABOUT THE AUTHOR

Violet Howe writes books about heroines who are at a crossroads or facing obstacles. Her stories have romance but also explore relationships with family and friends. Some of her books have a mystery, an element of suspense, or a ghost or two. Violet lives in Florida with her husband and three adorable but spoiled dogs. When she's not writing, Violet is usually watching movies, reading, or planning her next travel adventure. She believes in happily ever afters, love conquering all, humor being essential to life, and pizza being a necessity.

Newsletter

Visit www.violethowe.com to subscribe and be the first to know about Violet's new releases, giveaways, sales, and appearances.

Facebook Group

You can also find out about joining Violet's Facebook Reader Group, the Ultra Violets.

facebook.com/VioletHoweAuthor

twitter.com/Violet_Howe

instagram.com/VioletHowe

amazon.com/author/violethowe

bookbub.com/authors/violet-howe

THANK YOU

Thank you so much for taking the time to read this book. The longer I "reside" in Cedar Creek, the more stories I find to be told, and you, dear reader, make it so much more fun for me to bring them to life. I read one time that a story begins in the mind of the author and ends in the mind of the reader, but I think that with us both sharing the experience, the story and the characters are able to live on indefinitely, and I thank you for that.

If you liked this book, then please tell somebody! Tell your friends. Tell your family. Tell a co-worker. Tell the person next to you in line at the grocery store.

If you really liked it, please consider reviewing it on BookBub, Goodreads, your favorite online vendor, or any other social media site you frequent.

www.ingramcontent.com/pod-product-compliance
Lightning Source LLC
Chambersburg PA
CBHW071409100726
47908CB00004B/1111